Milly and the Memory Bank

a milly buntly adventure

milly MEMORY & the BANK

Angus Macdonald

Spiderwize

Milly and the Memory Bank

Spiderwize
Office 404, 4th Floor
Albany House
324/326 Regent Street
London
W1B 3HH
UK

www.spiderwize.com

Cover illustration by Toby Atkins

ISBN: 978-1-908128-10-2

Contents

1 Family Life

This is the most amazing story. I mean, lots of stories are cool. Like when I was little I loved Cinderella and when I was really, really little it was all about The Elves and the Shoemaker. You know, stories that end happily where nice people always come out on top. Now I'm twelve I like more grown up stories where you can't tell which characters are good and not everything works out for the best. But this is the most amazing story. And I'm actually in it, along with my little brother Jonas and our dog Moses. We're the good characters. Don't worry, you'll meet the baddies soon enough.

It's probably best to start at the beginning. We were on our usual family run, a trip to the Recycling Centre followed by a trip to the Memory Bank and then the supermarket. Just a normal Saturday, until Jonas found the business card at the Memory Bank. Okay, so it's obvious now the card was placed as a way of contacting Jonas. And Jonas, being the sensible sort, wanted nothing to do with it. So it was up to me to call the number. This threw us into a world where people couldn't be trusted, it was tricky telling good from bad, and everything we did had serious consequences. A world we're still in, though Jonas doesn't know this yet.

*

Except now I think back, it wasn't such a normal Saturday after all. Because a normal Saturday would see me lugging Jonas' load of Slam bottles for recycling and Jonas helping Dad carry the few twigs and leaves they collected from the garden. Well, this particular Saturday I'd had enough of all that and put my foot down.

'But we've been through this a million times already,' said Dad, hurriedly loading the car with the Slam bottles I left in the house. 'Jonas is too little to reach the slot for bottles and he helps out more in the garden in the first place.'

'But it's not fair,' I said. 'Ever since he won that competition giving him free Slam juice for a whole year, the amount we recycle has skyrocketed and I've loads more to do than anyone else.'

'Just the luck of the draw, I'm afraid, darling,' said Mum.

'Why don't you swap with me then, Mum, or at least stop Jonas drinking so much Slam juice? I'm sure it's not very good for him.'

'You know fine well it's the healthiest juice on the market. You also know the more Jonas drinks the more funding the Noors get in Sumatra.'

'Yeah, yeah, so the more coffee Dad gets for free in return.'

'Darling, it's not about that, and you know it isn't. Please don't make this morning any more difficult than it already is. Now let's just go or we'll be late.'

It was true that Mum wasn't having such a very good day, after another of her tussles with Moses. You see, Mum likes to make stuff and Moses got hold of one of her 'creations'.

'Lucky children,' people say when they hear she designs clothes.

'Yeah, but.'

'Good with a needle and thread then,' people say.

'Not bad.'

Mum makes clothes of very high quality that fit beautifully and last ages. Great if you lived in the decade when Mum was young. Baggy trousers you could hide Moses under, brightly coloured jumpers with digital shapes running across them, smiley t-shirts: these clothes might have been cool when Mum was my age, but that was thirty years ago and she's now well past forty.

You're probably wondering how Moses can hide under a trouser leg but he's a really tiny dog you see, a three-year-old Affenpinscher with a shaggy black coat. The thing he loves above all is to get out into the garden and dig things up. Moses is never happier than when covered in dirt and mud, which he trails through the house. This really upsets Mum, but if you asked Moses he'd say it's the best thing ever because he'd lead you to the treasure trove of things he's dug up.

Anyway, as I said, Moses was the reason Mum wasn't having such a great day. Every now and then Mum makes Moses some little toy to play with, which pretty much involves him burying it one day and digging it up the next. Only Moses got confused that morning and buried the new doll Mum made for Baby Ellen.

Baby Ellen is Mum's little brother Uncle Stan's daughter. She's sixteen months old and truly the noisiest, messiest, most annoying little baby cousin you could ever have the misfortune of being related to.

So Mum sat Moses down and 'had words with him'.

'Now Moses,' she said, in her softest, gentlest voice, 'you know you've been a naughty boy and hidden the doll Mummy made for Ellen.'

Just then a fly went past Moses' nose and he bounded off in pursuit.

'Moses,' Mum said, her voice rising as her control over the situation vanished. 'Moses, come back, Moses boy, come back.'

You'll soon learn this is a typical event in the Buntly household. If you ask me, Mum having a word with Moses never does either of them any good. This is because Moses has a different agenda from Mum, being a dog and all, but I'm not sure either of them fully realise it. It's certainly fair to say Moses often makes out that he's listening to Mum and paying attention. The problem is he'll then go and do the exact opposite of what it is Mum wants.

*

We finally got to the Recycling Centre around midday, where Mum's cardboard and paper, Dad and Jonas do gardening waste and I'm bottles and cans. Except today Dad's garden waste *and* bottles and cans and I sit in the car and watch. So Jonas' silly obsession of getting as much out of his offer as one small, very irritating boy can manage means Dad now has to make two additional trips between the car and the bottle bank. And get his hands sticky because Jonas never drains the bottles properly (what's the point, he says) and never ever rinses them out before dropping them into one of the extra extra-large size bags they're collected in. The reason for Dad's enthusiasm, of course, is that recycling Slam bottles really improves our Environmental Account, so we get lots more funding to help the Noors. And helping the Noors means free coffee for Dad, sent directly from their plantation in Sumatra.

Which is just as well, because the amount of coffee Dad drinks would totally ruin our Health Account. Health Accounts estimate the amount of healthy stuff like fruit and vegetables you put in your shopping trolley compared to unhealthy stuff like sweets or alcohol. The more unhealthy stuff you put in your trolley now, the less you are allowed to buy in the future until your Health Account balances itself out again. To use an extreme example, the Rumple family had such a calorie rich Health Account they were restricted to a diet of lentils and Brussels sprouts for a month before even being allowed to buy a single low calorie packet of biscuits and some organic tea leaves. How do I know this? Because their story is plastered all over the billboard outside the supermarket entrance, besides the Ascot family smiling up at the two extra solar panels installed on their roof for having the healthiest Health Account in the district.

Ever since the government withdrew paper money so that everything goes on your identity card, the only safe way to get stuff that's bad for you is through the black market. Unfortunately the black market works for some people better than others. Boys like Marcus Watt, for instance. Last Thursday Marcus spent the entire morning break flashing a packet of Knick-Knacks around the school playground telling anyone who'd listen that his dad, a barber, got a box of them by giving free haircuts to the supplier. This was before Bruce Boyd, known as Banana Bruce because he's got yellow hair and is very slippery, grabbed the Knick-Knacks, stamped on them and threw them into the bin, causing Marcus to burst into tears. I must admit I was more on the side of Banana Bruce than Marcus Watt. I suppose the black market is all very well if your mum or dad has a useful job like plumbing or hairdressing, but I don't think anybody wants old fashioned clothes or what it is Dad does for a living.

Between recycling and shopping we went to the Memory Bank. Jonas and me are on the first floor, one up from the infant floor, which is for children from 3 to 7. Babies and children under 3 are forbidden after government research into Memory Banks found that little children confuse authentic and virtual memories. You see, at that age children are more a bunch of memories than their own little selves, so virtual memories can have a harmful effect on their development.

I think this is sensible, especially after what happened to Amy in Primary 2. Her mummy took her to the Memory Bank before these government warnings were issued. Amy was barely two and not yet out of nappies when she experienced a forty-two-year-old weather presenter's virtual memory of his celebrations following a successful job interview at the BBC. Nobody really knows what happened during this virtual memory because it was downloaded by Amy before ViMs, as virtual memories are known, were recorded. In fact, it took a team of consultants three weeks of trawling through hours of taped interviews with Amy to piece together what the ViM was even about. After all, you wouldn't immediately connect a weather presenter's wild night out at the

Tropicana club in the West End of London with thoughts of finding new ways of using a potty, or whatever it is two-year-olds think about. All anybody knows is that Amy has not been the same since.

Dad is unsympathetic about this.

'Common sense should tell Amy's mum her daughter was too little for a ViM. I mean they wouldn't go to see a PG or 12 in the cinema, would they? You tell me how Memory Banks are any different. Especially in the early days, when the industry was run by cowboys and Indians.'

'Dad, you can't say that any more. They're Native Americans.'

'Right, and I'm Chief Wampum Woo. But I still think the industry needs more legislation.'

'More what, Daddy?'

'More rules. You know, maybe more research into the kinds of people allowed to upload memories.'

It's very unlike Dad to want more rules about anything, but I see his point. I mean, I haven't had any bad experiences with ViMs, but I've heard of people who have.

I actually had a very pleasant ViM that day. One of the things about the Memory Bank that people like is the way it makes you look at your own life from a different angle. Because you have to upload a memory in order to download one, you spend a lot of time thinking about the kinds of memories you'd like to use and which category they should go in. Memories are stored in five categories: Self Esteem Memories, Life Changing Memories,

Family Memories, Fun Memories and Adventure Memories. Half have to be in the same category of memory you've uploaded and half can be in a category of your choosing. This is because the kind of people who want a Self Esteem Memory might not have much self-esteem and users interested in Family Memories might be alone in life. But the real success of the service is that no matter what kind of memory you put in you'll usually get a ViM that is equal to it or better. That way everybody wins.

Jonas has a patchy record with the Memory Bank. His good downloads are some of the best I know, but his bad downloads are easily the worst. This might be because his uploads are also very hit and miss. Anyway, the one I want to tell you about he calls the Scary Man ViM, which he uploaded two weeks before we found the business card.

Jonas Buntly is alone on a beach at night. We are in Indonesia, which is a hot country, and he is wearing his swimsuit and a sarong, which he got from the Noors and thinks smells of coffee. He's had a relaxing day swimming in the sea and playing and is just dropping off to sleep. He should be in bed but he managed to sneak out and reckons what his parents don't know won't hurt them.

Suddenly there's a great crack in the air followed by a steady rumbling as though the ground he's sitting on is hungry. Jonas looks out and sees the moon and stars darken. He looks over to the two small islands on the horizon, all that remain of the larger volcanic island of Krakatoa, and sees traces of smoke rising from them. Krakatoa must be having a little tummy rumble. This is all Jonas has time to think about before something tells him to look over his right shoulder.

Where the sand meets the palm trees, he sees a figure dressed like a monk walking slowly towards the beach house where he's staying. Immediately Jonas feels frightened. Another hundred yards and the figure will be between Jonas and the room he's sleeping in. The air carries a chill and he feels Goosebumps spread over his body. Something about the movement of the figure tells Jonas it's not of this world and that he should stay rooted to the spot. His heart beats and his head spins. The figure then walks behind a tree directly in line between where he's sitting and his bedroom. He waits for it to reappear, but it doesn't. It just seems to vanish. What's happened? Is it hiding behind the tree waiting for Jonas to walk past so it can grab him, or has it simply melted into the hot night? Jonas sits in pure terror for his life for a long time before running as fast as he can over the sand past the tree to his room. He doesn't look left or right or back or stop until he's on the other side of his bedroom door and it's securely locked.

Don't ask me how Jonas got this weird memory into his head. I hardly remember the trip we made to see the Noors in Indonesia four years back, and Jonas would have only been six. For instance, I just thought we flew home directly after visiting the Noors. But it seems we went to this beach resort first.

It sure makes for a pretty exciting upload though, doesn't it? And a useful one too, because I got an extra Slam juice out of Jonas for promising not to give Mum and Dad the transcript showing he'd been out of his room in the middle of the night in a foreign country. Not to mention the central importance it's played in our lives since. You see it's because of this ViM that Thomas Fiskdale left his business card in Jonas' capsule.

2 Frenchman

As it happens, Jonas also had a good experience at the Memory Bank on the day we found the business card. In fact, he feels his visits are improving now he has a better understanding of how it works, though he gets frustrated by the limited number of ViMs allowed in the same category. His way around this is to save up same category ViMs for a month in order to have an entire run of them the next. And his category of choice is always the same: Family.

This is because Jonas believes he's an orphan. In other words, he thinks Mum and Dad aren't *really* his mum and dad and I'm not *really* his big sister. Crazy, isn't it. His evidence for this is based on three things: his hair is red, there are no photographs from the day he was born although there are lots from the day I was born and he's good at French. It's still not immediately clear? Well, let me try to explain things the Jonas way.

Ever since he was little Jonas has stood out in family photographs like a beetroot in a field of cabbages. This image is Jonas's, not mine. In fact fields of beetroots and fields of cabbages look very much alike as they both have green leaves and the actual edible part of the beetroot grows underground. I know because I went to Google Images to check it out.

Whenever he mentions his hair colour Jonas is told both his Great Granddad on Mum's maternal side and his Great Granny on Dad's paternal side had red hair. The family photograph album is then brought out and he is shown their pictures… in black and white.

'Case closed,' says Jonas, in his annoying way.

As to there being no photographs of the day Jonas was born, the fact is there are, but they're not the kind Jonas wants to see. This is because they're not taken in a hospital ward like the photographs of the day I was born. Why? For one very simple reason: Jonas was born at home. But this isn't enough for Jonas. He has done a comparison of newborn pictures and claims he has too much hair to be a newborn and the shots were taken after he'd been brought round to Mum and Dad from the orphanage.

'But some newborns do have a lot of hair, Jonas,' Mum explains patiently.

'Again it goes back to the hair,' says Dad, less patiently.

'I just want to know who I really am, n'est pas,' says Jonas in his best French accent.

'Jonas, I'm letting you know I'm finding this really hurtful,' says Mum.

'Come on, son,' says Dad more gently, holding Mum's hand, appealing to whatever family feeling Jonas still has.

'Non, je ne regrette rien,' says Jonas, which is French for saying he doesn't care. He picked up this expression from a song by a woman called Edith Piaf Mum used to play in the car. It's at moments like this I wish I could ring Jonas' neck, or at least throw a basket of rotten cabbages over him.

It is true that Jonas is unusually good at French, though. His favourite subject is French and his favourite teacher is Mme Flaubert, who told Mum and Dad proudly that he is the first ten-year-old she's met who can count to a hundred in French *backwards*. He reads French language comics like Tintin and Asterix. He collects French stamps and old French currency from the time before Euros. When we go out he asks for French mustard to go with his meal and Perrier or Evian water to drink. He supports Les Bleus, as the French football and rugby teams are called, and wears a scarf with Allez France written on it when the matches are shown on TV. His favourite food is French Fries. His favourite shop is French Connection. He even says he once French kissed a girl called Sophie from his class, though I don't believe him.

The reason for all this is obvious to Jonas: he's actually French, but a British family adopted him due to some terrible mix-up at the orphanage.

Luckily for Jonas, when it comes to the Memory Bank, he has a stock of French memories to draw on because for the past three years we've gone to the same campsite in France for our summer holidays. Now he's stored up his same category ViMs, all he has to do is upload something from one of these holidays in the hope of getting a related download that might confirm his Frenchness.

That week's upload was set on a Cross Channel ferry coming back from France. I know many people use the Channel Tunnel to make this journey, but Mum is frightened of tunnels so we always take the ferry. Jonas was wearing his Allez France scarf and this was spotted by a French boy his age called Paul who needed a partner for a game of table football he'd set up against Les Anglais.

Now I'm sure if this were a group of girls, the fact that Jonas was actually from Danemore and not Dieppe, the French port we'd just left, would be immediately obvious. But in my experience boys are not very observant types, especially when they're busy playing silly games. As a result Jonas was able to spend what he calls the happiest twenty minutes of his life playing table football on the French team with a real French boy from France against a couple of Birmingham City supporters from Kidderminster called Keith and Nigel. Jonas, or Zidane, as Paul Christened him, managed to keep up the illusion by carefully copying everything Paul said after practising the way it sounded in his head first.

'Incroyable,' Paul said after they went one nil up.

'Incroyable,' Jonas Zidane said after they scored their second.

'Zut alors,' Paul said after Les Anglais made the score 2-1.

'Zut alors,' Jonas Zidane said after Les Anglais equalised with their second.

'Incroyable,' Paul said again when the score became 9-7.

'Incroyable,' Jonas Zidane repeated after scoring the winning goal to make the final score 10-7.

'It's like playing against a funny French parrot,' Nigel complained as Paul gave Jonas a bear hug that ended with them rolling around on the floor in celebration.

You're probably wondering why Jonas entered this upload in the family section. Well, when the winners separated to rejoin their families as the ferry approached Newhaven, Jonas was clearly able to make out a 'mon frere' among the jumble of words Paul bid him farewell with. An actual French boy had called Jonas his brother with real warmth after they'd worked together to defeat Les Anglais. What further proof was needed of Jonas' true identity?

Dad says life's all a question of how you look at it. Jonas uploaded this Family Memory as confirmation of his strongest feelings. I think it's more like a cry for help from a very confused little brother and look forward to normal service resuming, though normal service will never resume with Jonas for the very simple reason that it never started in the first place. The return download didn't support his case either, but he didn't mind because it was set in Paris Disneyworld, which Jonas gets very excited about since even discussing the prospect of visiting it was banned a few years back. Dad says this is because the Walt Disney Company setting up a theme park in the heart of Europe is 'a sign of American Imperialism at its worst' but Jonas and I think it's because he doesn't want to pay the fifty Euro surcharge for campervans.

It was after Jonas had finished the download and was climbing out of the Memory Bank unit that he noticed a small rectangular card sticking out between the side of the mattress and the capsule wall. Jonas' first thought was that previous users' belongings getting left behind like this was clear evidence the units weren't cleaned after use. He even thought he got a whiff of something funny coming from the pillow. Standards were slipping. He must remember to choose a different capsule next week, break his habit of using the same one each time. He queued up to make a complaint at the information desk, but decided against it after reading what was written on the card.

Thomas Fiskdale
Meteorologist
Tel: 0778 568532
Email: T.Fiskdale@bbc.co.uk

'What do you think?' he asked anxiously after I'd read it once we got home from the supermarket. The only other time I'd ever seen him look this serious was immediately after he discovered he'd mistaken Moses' dog food for pate and spread it all over his French bread.

I told him I had no idea what he was talking about and why was this a big deal anyway. Even astronauts had to live somewhere when they're not out exploring meteors so why not in Danemore. It's a perfectly nice place with good parks and playgrounds and a leisure centre people travel from right across the county to visit.

'No, no, no,' said Jonas. 'That's not what a meteorologist is, silly. Meteorologists are the people who give the weather report. They're weather presenters. So what would a meteorologist's card be doing in a capsule on our floor of the Memory Bank?'

'Oh, I don't know. Maybe it's the weather person's son and he was playing with it before a download started and dropped it and the cleaner missed it. Maybe it was left over from the old Memory Bank. Who knows?'

And frankly, Jonas, who cares?

'Maybe, maybe, maybe... Too many maybes there, sis. C'mon, Milly, think. Remember what happened to Amy in P2.'

'You mean when she came out talking funny and has never been the same since.'

'Exactly. Now what was that download about?'

'Something she was too young for because it was for grown ups.'

'Yeah. But what was it about?'

'A man celebrating something by doing something naughty.'

'Celebrating what.'

'That he just got the job he wanted.'

'As.'

'As a weather presenter.'

'Exactly, Milly. Exactly. As a weather presenter, also known as a meteorologist. Working at the BBC. Now, why don't you have another look at the card?'

After much discussion we agreed there was a very good chance the uploader of the memory affecting Amy could be the meteorologist on the card. After all, how many meteorologists lived in Danemore? And how many meteorologists living in Danemore used the Memory Bank? The question now was what to do about it. Jonas wanted to do nothing because he thought Mr Fiskdale might be scary and would become a lot scarier when he discovered we'd found his card where it shouldn't have been.

'We should at least report it to the Memory Bank,' I said. 'Hand it over to the authorities and explain what happened to Amy and that this man might have something to do with it.'

Jonas looked unsure. I picked up my mobile and called directory enquiries to find out the number for the Memory Bank.

'C'mon, Jonas, we owe it to Amy.'

Now I'm ashamed to say that what I said to Jonas I was doing and what I actually did was just the *tiniest* little bit different. But at least it proves once and for all that Jonas never intended to get involved, in case we run into trouble in the future and he gets the blame. Instead of dialling the number for Danemore Memory Bank that directory enquiries gave me I entered Mr Fiskdale's number into my phone. The phone rang and rang and I was beginning to think nobody would answer when I heard a strangely familiar voice.

'Hello. Thomas Fiskdale speaking. How can I help you?'

I had to be careful because I could tell Jonas was listening.

'Yes. Hello there. This is Milly Buntly. I'd like to report a lost card that I found in a Memory Bank unit.'

Mr Fiskdale's tone became immediately warmer.

'Hello, Milly. Good to hear from you. I was looking forward to talking with you, although I must say I was expecting a boy. Must have a word with Giles about misuse of the facilities, eh.'

I was glad to hear Thomas Fiskdale didn't sound scary at all.

'Yes, well, I just thought you should know we found it in the children's section.'

'Indeed you did. I suspect there's somebody in the room with you, so we'll keep it short. You see, I have a proposal for you, Milly. When would be a good time to meet?'

3 Holbalm Hall

Holbalm Hall, where Thomas Fiskdale lived, was bigger than Danemore Primary School. It was bigger than Danemore High School. It was bigger than Danemore Castle and bigger than Danemore Hospital and very possibly bigger than Danemore Castle and Danemore Hospital put together. In fact, it was the biggest building I had ever seen. Which made it all the stranger to discover that it was on a normal road three stops from school. How had I never noticed it before?

It took ten minutes to walk from the corner of Holbalm Hall, where the bus let me off, to the front door. Holbalm Hall took up the whole of one side of the road and I must have passed dozens of houses across from it. It was a blisteringly hot afternoon, but the building blocked out so much of the sun I had to put my school jumper on after turning into the road. The weather presenter's house was so large it changed the climate of the entire area.

The front door was ordinary though, just like every other front door in the street. It was even a little shabby looking, with the red paint all chipped and leaves piled up on the doorstep. I pressed the buzzer and heard the crackle of lightning followed by three thunderclaps and the sound of heavy rain. Well, I thought, this must be the right address then.

The door opened and a tall, thin man I immediately recognised from the TV offered his hand. I've heard it said famous people turn out to be shorter in real life, but Thomas Fiskdale was far larger and thinner and paler, so much so that he resembled a giant spider in his dark clothes.

'Welcome to Holbalm Hall, Milly,' he said. 'So glad you could make it. Come inside.'

It was the strangest thing. The hallway and kitchen was no different from that of a normal house's. It would have been rude to say anything, but I must have looked puzzled because Mr Fiskdale gave me an explanation after we'd sat down at the kitchen table.

'Messy divorce, I'm afraid, Milly. Something I hope you never have to go through. The lawyers took me to the cleaners and I had to make arrangements for all the rooms. The ballroom, master bedrooms, stables, cinema and gym: gone. All gone. So now I'm left with a two up two down, as I understand these hovels are called. And the façade. I was able to hold on to that for appearance's sake, though it pays havoc with the council tax.'

'What about the rest of it?'

'All virtual, I'm afraid. Just as you can have virtual memories, so you can also have virtual buildings. The technology is still in its development stage, so the general public don't know about it yet.'

'Amazing.'

'Scandalous, I'd say. Not to worry, Milly. I intend to get it all back, which is where you come in. Cup of tea, dear, or are you too young for the elixir of life?'

'Hold on. Where have all the rooms gone then?'

'The ballroom is currently being used in an exclusive private club in London so its elderly members can cha-cha-cha and Foxtrot to their heart's content. A rather famous footballer took the gym and swimming pool, presumably so he can work on his game, or whatever it is famous footballers do. The stables and library have been installed in a Russian billionaire's mansion near Exeter and the cinema replaced a rather forlorn Odeon situated between the public baths and bingo hall of a well known London high street.'

'Wow.'

'Wow indeed, Milly. The users have put down a considerable deposit in case anything is damaged or in any way different from how it was at the point of sale. The rooms are pawned really, you see, and I've got a buy back clause for when I get the necessary funds together. The rooms they are replacing had to be exactly the same dimensions so that nothing was squashed or stretched in the move. This was the only condition really, though it made the whole thing a bit of a logistical nightmare, I'm afraid. As I said, the technology is still in the early stages.'

'So it's like the TARDIS, only the other way round.'

'Indeed. Now, shall we get down to business?'

Mr Fiskdale unlocked a filing cabinet and started pulling pieces of paper out.

'I'd like to buy the license to one particular Memory Bank upload from you.'

'I didn't know you could buy licenses to people's memories.'

'Milly, in this life you can buy anything. Biscuit?'

'My dad says you should never take anything from somebody you don't know.'

'I see,' said Mr Fiskdale, pausing to reflect. 'I have an idea then. What if I show you the packet before putting it out on a plate? Would that satisfy you?'

I wasn't really talking about biscuits when I said this, but I'm glad Mr Fiskdale got the wrong idea because he took me into a cupboard. It was like entering the kind of sweet shop I remember visiting when I was a little girl before the new laws came in and they all had to close down. The cupboard was about half the size of the kitchen but there was only room for one person because it was so full of sweetie jars and multi-packs of snacks and nibbles and boxes of biscuits and crisps and cans of juice and a hundred other things that were yummy and bad for you and would destroy your Health Account in a blink. It was without a doubt the most magical room I had ever seen in my life and I immediately decided that I never wanted to leave.

'I have the privilege of being the UK representative of Homemaker Industries, America's leading chocolate and confectionary manufacturer,' Mr Fiskdale said, smiling. 'Now, what would you like?'

I left Holbalm Hall half an hour later with a belly full of lovely sickly sugary things, pockets crammed with sweets and a school bag stuffed with crisps and biscuits and all the kinds of things that either melt or explode when you put them in your mouth. All the things never allowed because of the damage done to your Health Account, if you were even able to source them in the first place.

I had so much stuff on me Mr Fiskdale decided the safest way to get home was to order a taxi. I also left with a deal that he would do his best to try and help Amy in exchange for the license to Jonas' Scary Man ViM. Ideally I'd have spent a lot longer at Holbalm Hall poking through the pantry, but Mum and Dad were expecting me back from a trip to the cinema with my friend Daisy in twenty minutes.

Once dinner was finished I went about completing my part of the bargain, transferring the license of the Scary Man ViM from Jonas to Mr Fiskdale. I wanted to do this ASAP because Mr Fiskdale said I could get the same amount of sweeties again and he'd try to help Amy. This was a win-win situation and I was really excited. But I immediately hit a stumbling block. Transferring the license wasn't as easy as Mr Fiskdale said it would be.

First I typed my name and passport to access the family account and open up the folder containing our personal files. Here the five of us- Mum, Dad, Jonas, Moses and me- were. I couldn't resist having a quick look at our Health and Environmental Accounts before focussing on Jonas' file. Everything looked really good there, especially since we were well on our way to meeting our government targets for the year and it was only May. There was a blip on the Health Account because of recent troubles Dad had with Baby Ellen when he took her out for the day, but I couldn't see that continuing after Dad had cut all contact with Baby Ellen's mum Auntie Mel afterwards. Other than this, everything was looking really good for the Buntly household.

Next I opened Jonas' file and went to his Memory Bank cache, where all his uploads were itemised and dated and subdivided into the five different categories for easy reference. Here it was: the Adventure upload of May the second. I had a quick read through to check.

Jonas Buntly is alone on a beach at night.

Blah, blah, blah. Perfect. Now it was simply a question of sending it over to Mr Fiskdale before pulling the license out. Open email, reply, add attachment, find file, highlight and click, send. Off it goes.

Now select the file in the hard drive. Nothing happens. A message pops up.

This file is locked. Please contact the license owner for assistance.

Okay, slight problem.

I decide there's only one thing to do. Go round Jonas' room with a bag of sweets and get him to give up the license to his Scary Man ViM. Shouldn't be too tricky because I'm sure it's one of the memories he'd rather forget about anyway. Unfortunately this involves having to admit that I wasn't entirely truthful about what I did after he showed me Mr Fiskdale's card. Better make it two bags, including his favourite liquorice ones. Oh, and as a result of which I'd gone round to see Mr Fiskdale personally, again without telling him. And maybe a few packs of Spider Webs, the BBQ Chicken flavour ones he really likes.

I know Jonas though: Jonas the conspiracy theorist, Jonas the man of principal and action, Jonas the argumentative-ask-a-million-questions-pain-in-the-neck. It would never work. Offering half the sweeties would never work. Offering *all* the sweeties would never work. Neither would offering all the sweeties now and all of the next lot of sweeties too. He'd see them as his right anyway: his memory, his sweeties. No, I had to take a different approach, one that would get to the heart of Jonas, the very *essence*.

*

I knock on his door and wait for him to answer. I never usually do this because he can take up to ten minutes to make his room accessible to 'aliens', as he calls people in his room who are not Moses or him. This involves marking the position of every piece on the board of whatever game he is playing, which usually takes place on the floor to give Adam Danger, or Dangerboy as he calls his regular imaginary foe, enough space to sit down. In case the intruder accidentally knocks or stands on a piece, or whatever it is Jonas imagines could possibly go wrong with his sad little games. He marks all the cards or units he's using with a grid position and the user's initials (JB for Jonas Buntly; AD for Adam Danger). These are then put in storage, which are shoe boxes Jonas has painted silver and written random numbers on to look all 22nd century.

You see now why I usually just barge in, but on this occasion I wait for him to grant access. Finally he calls out 'Alien Visiting

Hours Open' in a voice that is meant to be extra-terrestrial but sounds like he comes from Wales.

'Evening, Jonas,' I say, all bright and merry. 'What if I told you I've found a way to make Dad stop drinking coffee?'

Getting straight to the point is probably the best strategy. Nice and easy, but straight to the point.

'Wow, Milly. That would be great.'

'Okay, now listen carefully. This might get a little complicated so you have to follow what I'm going to say.'

Especially as I'm not a hundred percent sure what I'm going to say myself.

'I just checked our account and we're well on our way to achieving this because of the problems Dad's been having with Baby Ellen. You know how Baby Ellen cries all the time until she gets what she wants and how she always wants cake and how Dad always ends up giving in to her. Well, I just looked at our Health Account and it turns out he's lost forty five credits because of this. Another forty five credits and he'll drop a Health band, which will make lots of problems for the whole family. Understand?'

Jonas nods eagerly.

'Good. Now, I've been doing a little research and you know what is worth exactly forty five credits? Or at least forty five credits in the crazy volume Dad drinks it? Coffee: a luxury Dad's lucky to get directly from the Noors, or he'd have to make the choice between alcohol and coffee to balance his Health Account like most normal people.

Hold that thought and let's switch over to the Environmental Account. What's the single biggest thing getting us the most credits? You know the answer because it annoys you so much. Slam juice bottles. Without them Mr Noors wouldn't get so much funding and probably wouldn't send Dad so much coffee.'

Jonas nods sadly.

'Now, here's my proposal. As you know, it's my job to recycle bottles and cans. In other words, it's up to me to ensure all those Slam bottles get recycled so Dad gets his coffee.'

Jonas bounces up and down on the floor and continues my plan.

'Okay,' he says, 'so you stop recycling Slam bottles. Better yet, you trade them for sweeties and things, which is only fair because they're mine anyway. Genius. And Dad's left with a tough decision. He buys his own coffee, which drops us all down a Health band, or he gives up coffee entirely. Genius.'

I couldn't have put it any better myself. Now it was just a case of explaining to Jonas that I'd complete my part of the bargain and trade Slam bottles on the open market at great personal risk if he'd just do one *tiny* teeny weenie thing for me.

4 Milly's Misstep

You thought my next move was to ask Jonas to give me the password to his Memory Bank account, didn't you? Admittedly it crossed my mind, but only until I had a far better idea. Or what I thought was a better idea at the time. When I say it involved both Marcus Watt, the biggest scam artist in the history of Danemore Primary School, and Moses, you'd never guess who was responsible for it falling apart so disastrously. Or maybe you would, and I'm just being dumb. When you think about it, Marcus knows all about keeping secrets. But Moses doesn't because, well, because he's a dog.

I just felt there was a risk of Jonas kicking up a storm when I asked him for his password. He wouldn't rest until he'd needled everything out of me. Where would that leave us? I mean, the whole thing with Mr Fiskdale was obviously very fishy. At the same time, what he did with Jonas' upload and why he wanted it was really none of our business. Especially when we had all those sweets coming to us, and could help little Amy into the bargain. Wasn't that enough? But I knew it wouldn't be nearly enough for Jonas, who *likes to get to the bottom of things*.

So I came up with an alternative plan from Jonas' idea of trading Slam bottles for sweets. This, after all, could always be arranged, since the sweets were already here. All I needed was an accomplice, and who better than black marketer par excellence Marcus Watt. I could throw a little business his way and everybody would be happier and nobody would be any the wiser.

I made the deal with Marcus over lunchtime at school. He'd take Jonas away every week and give him my sweeties in exchange for fifteen Slam bottles. Marcus was dead keen on recycling ever since his family started sponsoring metal workers in the Xinjiang Province of China and the Chinese sent clippers and scissors for his dad's salon in return. All Marcus had to do was pretend the sweeties were payment for the bottles and meet Jonas in a location far enough away from our house to buy me half an hour. This half hour would be spent rummaging through Jonas' bedroom searching for his password, but I didn't tell him that bit and he didn't ask.

I see now the plan failed because I rushed into it. Five minutes after my conversation with Jonas the night before I got a text from Mr Fiskdale saying he was delighted with the transcript for the Scary Man upload and looking forward to receiving the hard copy. So I knew I had to get into Jonas' room for some serious rummaging ASAP. My mistake was to arrange for Marcus to meet Jonas before I had everything properly in place. I'd been clued up enough to take sweeties into school for Marcus to fob off on Jonas, but there was simply no way of getting fifteen Slam bottles to him undetected. So what to do with these Slam bottles in the meantime? Jonas would come back with his fistful of sweets and wonder why they were all still in their extra extra-large size bags ready to go to the Recycling Centre. And I still might have got away with it but for the fact that if there's one thing everybody knows about Marcus Watt, it's that he doesn't do deals until he has what it is you're trading with him first.

I rushed back from school with my work cut out. Marcus guaranteed me a twenty five minute window before Jonas got home and I had to dispose of fifteen Slam bottles and still have time for some rummaging, which was the whole point of striking the deal with him in the first place. Then it came to me. Who better to help me than Moses, the greatest burier of stuff known to man?

*

I'd just had my first unsuccessful rummage through Jonas' bedroom and was wondering what to text back to Mr Fiskdale when I heard noises downstairs. Immediately I feared the worst and rushed down in the hope that my presence would have some influence on events. I was half way down the stairs when the horrible reality hit home.

Mum had her back to me in the hallway. She held Moses in one arm and wielded a Slam bottle in the other to defend him with. Moses had a grubby snout and looked very pleased, wagging his tail and barking furiously. Between them and the front door was Dad, leaping up and down on the spot, fists raised like a boxer, shouting abuse at Moses. Jonas just got home and stood in his coat holding an empty packet of Swizzlesticks and looking confused. Fourteen grass covered Slam bottles were stacked neatly down one side of the hallway.

'Quelle catastrophe', as Jonas might say, which is what the French exclaim when things go wrong.

The mistake I'd made was to fall for the old Mum trap of believing Moses understood anything of what I was telling him. I'd given him clear instructions about what to do and popped a chocolate into his mouth every time I felt we were making progress and to reward him for good listening skills. I was so desperate for this to work I'd totally forgotten Moses was simply a dog playing a new game. And we were playing a new game, I suppose, though only one of us was following the rules. The rule of the game was simple: hide fifteen Slam bottles in the grass cuttings until new orders are given. Moses version of the game was to hide fifteen Slam bottles in the grass cuttings and then immediately dig them up again, before arranging them in a line in the hallway. Which was an entirely different game that had no resemblance to the one I wanted us to play. Oh well.

'That dog has been trouble ever since he arrived,' Dad was saying to Mum.

'That dog has got a name, Desmond. Please use it.'

'Very well, then,' said Dad. 'Moses has been a pain in our backsides from the moment he walked through the door.'

'Language, Desmond. Remember: little ears,' said Mum, pointing at Jonas with the Slam bottle.

'It's just as well he's present to hear all this,' said Dad. He turned to face Jonas. 'Jonas, it's just as well you're present to hear all this. And where have you been for the last half hour?'

'Out,' said Jonas.

'I can see that, thank you, Jonas. Where out have you been? Oh, never mind. I'm getting away from my point.'

'And what is your point exactly, Desmond?'

'My point, my point? Do I even have to make it when the evidence is all lined up before you? That dog, Moses, has proved once again he's completely out of control. After all the time and money invested in making him feel at home. After the hours of training we've put in, teaching him routines, modelling good behaviour. And this is the thanks we get.'

Dad starts flinging his arms around like a wild man, but Mum keeps her cool and a tight control of Moses, the Slam bottle and the situation.

'Three points, Desmond. First of all, *we* didn't put in the training, *I* put in the training. Secondly, I just had a quick look at the bags of Slam bottles and don't think we've lost any. And thirdly, Moses is a dog, Desmond. He's a dog, not a robot. We love him for what he is. In any case, you're only upset because you worry about the effect fewer Slam bottles will have on the amount of coffee you get from the Noors.

Now you know my feelings about this in the first place. These bottles are Jonas' contribution, so by rights Jonas should have a say about what sorts of things we get back from Sumatra, especially since he hates your coffee habit and endlessly moans about it to me when it's got absolutely nothing to do with me. I read an article in the Sunday magazine recently about how very good swings and climbing frames are made out of bamboo, which is the Noors' other crop, as you well know.'

'Ooh yes please,' says Jonas, forgetting the deal he struck with Marcus.

'Now,' says Mum, 'lets Moses and Jonas and I wash these bottles and return them to the Recycling pile and forget all about this. Really, Desmond, what a fuss over nothing.'

*

This wasn't the end of it for me, of course. Jonas knew he'd found me out and would look to press his advantage for anything he could get. He had me in his sites and it was just a matter of time before closing in for the kill.

An hour later he entered my room uninvited and stood over my desk.

'Okay, sis,' he said, 'it's time to tell me what this is all about.'

I knew he meant business because he brought his main interrogation weapon, a bedside table alarm clock, with him. The first thing to do in these situations is act innocent. I casually look up from my maths homework and talk like my mind's still on it. It's good to have a prop handy for nervous hands, so I pick up my compass to play with, even though the page I'm working on doesn't need one.

'You know what Moses is like yourself.'

Delivered in the most neutral way I can manage. Like this has nothing to do with me and I can still see things from different viewpoints.

'I can understand Dad's frustration, but Mum's got a good point too and I'm sure it will all boil over. After all, no harm's been done.'

'Come on, sis. Don't play me the fool. You know what I'm talking about. Moses buried fifteen Slam bottles, which just so happens to be exactly the same number Marcus Watt is getting in exchange for sweets. Something's going on and you're going to tell me what it is.'

The second thing to do in these situations is confess a version of the truth. This version will only be effective if it serves two main purposes. Firstly, it hides the real reason behind your actions. Secondly, it puts your interrogator on the back foot by showing that this is all being done for him in the first place. It helps to act just a little narked at this stage.

'Yeah, well, I didn't have time to get them over to him, all right. Sorry, but I'm not a miracle worker. And you were so keen to get your precious sweets that I asked Marcus to wait a few days before I could safely get the bottles to him, which he agreed to because he really wants to recycle them for his dad. Meantime I had to hide them in case Dad had any bright ideas about recycling early or something. You know what Dad's like.'

'Oh, I know what Dad's like. I also know what you're like. You're up to something and I want you to tell me what it is. Everybody knows Marcus Watt doesn't do deals until he has what he wants first. He's the hardest nut to crack and not even you can crack him. So what's going on, sis? C'mon, tell me another one. I could do with a laugh.'

Jonas sits down on my spare chair, puts his feet up on the desk and starts the stopwatch on the alarm clock he's placed between us. He takes a packet of Monster Mash from out of his pocket and starts eating very slowly, popping them into his mouth one at a time to savour the flavour. He doesn't offer me one and points to the clock.

'I'm not going anywhere. We've got all night if we need it.'

Twenty minutes later I've confessed it was under my instruction that Moses hid the Slam bottles so Jonas would think they were already with Marcus Watt. Thirteen minutes after that I've admitted I was unable to get Marcus Watt to honour his part of the deal until he had something in return first. Following this I'm proud to say I was able to hold out a further twenty two minutes before admitting that what he already had was the sweets Jonas was currently munching his way through because, well, because they're actually mine in the first place. A full confession came very quickly after that. But at least I'd held out for most of an hour with the toughest griller in the business. And I never had to mention anything about rummaging through his room. In actual fact, I even got Jonas to agree to send Mr Fiskdale the ViM he wanted. There was only one condition. Jonas wanted to meet Mr Fiskdale first.

5 Jonas' Deal

'Mr Fiskdale, I'd like you to meet my brother Jonas.'

Mr Fiskdale appeared a little caught off guard opening his front door to see us standing there before him.

'Hello, young man,' he said after a pause, holding his hand out for Jonas to take, his smile seeming to freeze on his face, 'welcome to Holbalm Hall. Milly, good to see you again.'

He glanced out into the street for a moment before returning to us.

'But you both look cold. Come in, come in, warm yourself in the kitchen.'

The funny thing was neither of us was remotely cold on what was clearly one of the warmest days of the year. It was only later, when I thought about it, that I realised Mr Fiskdale simply wanted us out of public view ASAP. Which made perfect sense, considering what we went on to discover over the next twenty four hours.

'Good to see you again, Milly,' he repeated as we followed him into the house.

I'd already explained about Holbalm Hall to Jonas so he wouldn't irritate our host with lots of irrelevant questions, but this only made him even more suspicious.

'Just goes to show,' he said.

'What do you mean?'

'The man's got no money, which seems about right because I've not seen him on the telly for ages. People with no money quickly become desperate and try all sorts of crazy things.'

'S'pose so,' I said.

'Well *yeah*, just look at Jesse James,' said Jonas, who was reading a book about the American Wild West at the time.

We were now sat at the kitchen table in front of a tin of biscuits Mr Fiskdale had brought out from the cupboard. The biscuits looked scrummy and tasted even scrummier and reminded me what a good time I'd had on my last visit. I was a lot more nervous now, though, with Jonas here beside me. I just hoped he wouldn't mess things up like usually happens when you take him somewhere new. I really needed him to be on his best behaviour.

'What a pleasant surprise to see you both,' Mr Fiskdale said. 'I'm assuming your parents don't know you're here.'

We both nodded.

'And for what do I owe the pleasure of your company, young Jonas? But wait. Don't answer yet. Who's for a cup of tea, or are you not old enough to appreciate God's own sweet brew?'

'Okay, Fiskdale,' Jonas said, ignoring the pleasantries and getting straight to business, 'I'm here because the upload you're trying to get from my sister is actually mine. So you have me to deal with if you want it, not her.'

'I see,' said Mr Fiskdale, measuring Jonas' words carefully.

His manner changed after Jonas' directness and I sensed for the first time he might not be the cuddly figure he made himself out to be. Something about the way he looked at us, like he had things he wanted to be getting on with and our presence was preventing him from getting on with them. It was an uncomfortable feeling that didn't fill me with much confidence in Jonas' plan to renegotiate the deal I'd already struck, despite Jonas still being the legal owner of the copyright. I decided it was best to just sit tight and see what happened, and helped myself to another biscuit in the meantime.

'I see,' he said again. 'Well, it's good to see you both and meet the man with the memories so important to my research.'

He stood up.

'Would you kindly excuse me for a minute? Feel free to help yourself to biscuits. I won't be long.'

In fact Mr Fiskdale was gone for what felt like a very long time indeed. He was gone so long Jonas and me started wondering what to do and whether we might even have a quick peek around the house or maybe just go home to think up another plan or even forget all about our crazy adventure before it was too late. But Mr Fiskdale returned before we'd settled on one particular course of action. He was holding a tube containing a sheet of paper he carefully emptied out on the floor. This he unrolled over the kitchen table after clearing it of the stuff kitchen tables get covered in. He fixed the corners in place using jam jars and salt and pepper grinders and urged Jonas and me to gather round for a closer look.

'Here, my dear friends,' he said, his jolly manner returned, 'is a map of the world, but with a difference.'

He indicated several large red circles on the map with the handle of a wooden spoon he'd taken from one of the kitchen drawers.

'Now, what do you think these represent?'

'I don't know,' said Jonas.

'Shall I give you a clue? As you'll no doubt already be aware, I'm a Meteorologist. What is less well known is that my particular field of Meteorology is Vulcanology. Hands up who can tell me what that is.'

Jonas' hand shot up.

'Easy. That's the study of volcanoes. Vulcanologists are the people who try and predict when and where the earth will blow its top next. So these circles maybe identify where the next big blast will happen.'

Mr Fiskdale looked impressed, but not as impressed as I must have done. Then I remembered Jonas' Environmental Studies topic last term was Materials from Earth and he'd even made a poster of a cross section of a volcano with Mum's help as a homework project.

'Almost, Jonas,' he said, offering him a biscuit from the tin floating in the middle of the Atlantic Ocean. 'That's a very good answer, but it's not quite right. These circles actually represent the ten biggest volcanic eruptions in recorded history by number of lives lost.'

Mr Fiskdale used the wooden spoon to point out the area of the map he was talking about.

'Here we have Vesuvius, which left Pompeii hidden under lava and ash for close on two millennia. Not many people know this, but Vesuvius actually erupted twice, most famously in AD 79, but also in 1631, at the estimated combined loss of 43,000 lives. The other European volcano in the top ten is Mount Laki in Iceland, which killed roughly one quarter of that island's population in 1783 and caused untold devastation across Europe for the eight months it erupted in total. Moving south and crossing the Atlantic we have Mount Pelee in Martinque, which blew its top in 1902 at the loss of 29,000 lives.'

Mr Fiskdale then directed his spoon over the Caribbean and through Mexico to sketch a wide loop from Central and South America up through Indonesia and Japan via New Zealand and finally to Alaska and California.

'And all but one of the remaining seven volcanoes are found in what is known as the Ring of Fire, here, around the Pacific Ocean.'

'Because of tectonic plates sliding around and pushing each other,' Jonas said enthusiastically. He was really getting into this and I was relieved to see his attitude towards Mr Fiskdale slowly soften.

'Exactly right, Jonas. This accounts for Nevado del Ruiz in Colombia, Santa Maria in Guatemala, Mount Unzen in Japan and Mounts Tambora, Kelut and Galunngung in Indonesia. Of course, Indonesia is unlucky to be doubly cursed by sitting on two regions of great seismic activity, the other being the Alpide belt, which accounts for Krakatoa and the Indian Ocean earthquake of 2004 that created a tsunami killing almost a quarter of a million people across the region.

It is these Indonesian volcanoes that are my area of specialisation. Through looking at eruptions that have happened in the past I'm trying to identify patterns and similarities that will help us in the future. And this, Jonas, is where your upload to the Memory Bank comes in.'

'How?' asked Jonas, munching a biscuit.

'What we have found,' said Mr Fiskdale, 'is that the use of new technologies such as the Memory Bank gives us invaluable insights into what occurs during the earliest stages of volcanic eruptions.'

'But Jonas wasn't anywhere near Krakatoa when it erupted,' I said. 'I mean, he wasn't even born yet, none of us were. So how could people's memories be recorded in the Memory Bank of something that happened centuries ago?'

'Right. Excellent point, Milly. Now, permit me if you will to answer your question by asking another? Do you believe in the supernatural?'

'I do,' Jonas spluttered out, his mouth full of biscuit.

'Right,' said Mr Fiskdale. 'Presumably because of this very upload we're discussing. Am I right?'

'Yeah,' said Jonas, 'exactly. I saw that ghost four years ago. I *know* I did. And I never believe anything I don't see with my own eyes. Ask Milly if you don't believe me.'

'Right.'

'Actually,' Jonas said, 'all this is making me thirsty. Can I get some water please?'

Jonas kicked me on the shin under the table when Mr Fiskdale turned his back to pour him a glass of water from the tap.

'What?' I whispered.

He indicated with his eyes that I look over to the cupboard where Mr Fiskdale kept his stash of sweeties. I raised my eyebrows to show my annoyance and mouthed the words 'I know'. Typical Jonas to start causing problems just when we were getting to the most exciting bit. I was sure I mentioned the cupboard of sweeties to Jonas before, but maybe it had slipped my mind in all the excitement.

Mr Fiskdale returned with Jonas' water.

'Of course the fascinating thing about this is that yours is not the only upload in the Memory Bank involving unexplained apparitions near the site of earthquakes and volcanic eruptions.'

'Hah,' said Jonas, delighted that his experience was finally being taken seriously.

'A coincidence, I might humbly say, that would almost certainly have been missed were I not to have been going through all of the uploads situated close to such sites as a routine matter during the course of my research.'

'Sure,' said Jonas, 'brilliant.'

Jonas was now acting *too* keen. This worried me. If I knew my brother, he was up to something. But Mr Fiskdale must have noticed my concern and misread it, because he went on to explain that he had been given special license from the government to access all Memory Bank libraries due to the critical importance of his research.

'Now the thing is,' he went on, encouraged by Jonas' enthusiasm and my smiling at him to show that I accepted what he said, 'in order to conduct proper research into this phenomenon I need to do certain things to the files that are only available to the copyright holder.'

It was at this point that I expected Jonas to launch into his rant about how Mr Fiskdale's business card came to be in his Memory Bank capsule in the first place. Or what right Mr Fiskdale had to enter into negotiations with me when it wasn't my memory to negotiate with. Or any number of other totally irrelevant issues that would have taken us away from the main reason we were here. But he didn't do any of this.

'Right,' he said, 'so as the holder of this copyright thingy I'm in a strong position. If I don't give you the copyright you can't do what you need to continue your work.'

'Exactly,' said Mr Fiskdale.

'The first thing you can do then is forget all about whatever agreement you struck with Milly here.'

'Okay,' said Mr Fiskdale, 'understood.'

'The second thing you have to do is give me all the connected memories you just mentioned. These need to be ready and waiting for me to access over the next few weeks I visit the Memory Bank so I can check them out. The sooner this happens the better for you because I won't hand over my file until I've seen them all.'

Mr Fiskdale nodded to show that he was agreeable to this.

'And the third thing you have to do is let Milly and I have another raid of your sweetie cupboard to take home as many sweeties as we can carry in the taxi you are going to order for us.'

'What about poor Amy?' I said.

'And still help Amy in any way you can.'

'You've got yourself a deal,' said Mr Fiskdale, smiling and looking relieved. 'And I'm sure future volcano and earthquake victims will thank you for helping me continue my research on their behalf.'

'Yeah, whatever,' said Jonas.

Jonas' cool response to Mr Fiskdale mentioning the real victims in all this should maybe have raised as many alarm bells for him as they did for me, but he didn't seem to notice. Or at least he chose to ignore it. Instead he walked over to the cupboard.

'Now, you'd no doubt like to have a rummage around here. Let me just switch the light on.'

'Yeah,' said Jonas. 'But first tell me where your loo is. All this water has run right through me and I'm busting.'

*

'Wow,' I said in the back of the taxi on our way home, 'you did really well, Jonas. Much better than I thought. By the way, would you like a Pink Panda?'

I held out the bag for him but he waved away my offer and turned in the seat to look me straight in the eye.

'Of course, you do know everything you've heard this afternoon has been complete and utter rubbish.'

'Yeah, cool,' I said, searching through my bag for the pack of Strawberry Stacks I picked up before realising what he said. 'What? No. What are you talking about?'

'He's making it all up as he goes along. Can't you see that?'

'How do you mean? What about the map? The map's real. And these sweeties here,' I said, shaking the bag. 'They're real, aren't they? What more do you want?'

'Milly, do you want to help Amy or do you just want to stuff yourself with sweeties for the next month until you grow into a great big fat blob?'

'Well,' I said, thinking about this seriously for a moment, 'I'd quite like to do both, if that's okay with you. And what's wrong with that anyway?'

'Okay then, do you like being lied to?'

'People lie all the time, sometimes for good reasons, sometimes bad. What does it matter? What does any of this matter? It's about what we can get out of it for ourselves. And if we can help Amy into the bargain, all the more reason for giving Mr Fiskdale a hand.'

'Oh it matters,' said Jonas. 'It matters all right. And tomorrow we're going back to Holbalm Hall, but with one difference. Fiskdale won't know a thing about it. In fact, he won't even know we're there.'

Which, it turned out, he was *almost* right about.

6 The Secret Room

'Here we go. Just as I thought: right all along.'

Jonas thundered into my room as I was putting away the last of my share of the sweets behind an old baby pram I used to play with when I was little. It was a tricky operation as I was doing this half the way up a ladder by cramming everything between the top of my wardrobe and the ceiling. I'd finally managed to get the pram in front of the stash and looking like it had been there for years when Jonas entered and the whole lot clattered down.

'Hold on. Can't you knock first, Jonas? What is it now?'

'I've just called the BBC and I'm right. Fiskdale hasn't worked there for two years. Not only this but he was fired for some reason the person wouldn't tell me. I bet it's for something really bad. Anyway, it's all very fishy and just as I thought: Fiskdale is a desperate man, and probably dangerous too. We've really got to watch our step from now on.'

'Jonas,' I said, climbing down the ladder and kicking as many sweeties as I could out of view behind the little skirt thingy that went round my bed, 'let's get one thing straight. There won't *be* any 'from now on'. 'From now on' is over and there's no way I'm going back to Holbalm Hall. Not unless I get invited by Mr

Fiskdale personally, and only if he's willing to throw a lot more sweets my way for the trouble.'

'What do you mean?'

'Just what I said. After thinking about it, I've decided I agree with you about Mr Fiskdale being a weirdo. And I've no doubt Holbalm Hall is wired up to the nines with security to warn off burglars. These sorts of places always are.'

'Not any more,' said Jonas, looking pleased with himself.

'Oh Jonas, what have you done?'

'You know how I always carry a penknife on me in case of emergencies? Well, as soon as I saw there was something not right about Holbalm Hall I decided we had to go back and investigate, but this time without Fiskdale as our tour guide. So I fixed things up to make this possible.'

'But I told you about this already, Jonas. How rooms in Holbalm Hall were sold off and all that's left is a normal house. You knew about it before we even got there.'

'So you didn't catch what I was meaning when I kicked you under the kitchen table then?'

'I just thought you'd finally spotted what was in the cupboard.'

'But that's exactly what I mean. The cupboard should have been dark because the light was switched off. So how was I able to see inside it?'

'Easy. The light from the kitchen through the glass panel in the door.'

'Only this?'

'Yeah. Of course.'

'Shame. Because actually there was another light coming from inside the cupboard. Now, if you agree the cupboard light was off, where was this light coming from?'

'Beats me,' I said, already bored with the conversation and still seething with Jonas for messing up my hiding place.

'My bet is this cupboard leads to a secret room and it's the light from this we saw. Who knows, there are maybe loads of secret rooms. How long did it take us to walk from the bus stop to the front door? We couldn't see inside because of the big wall all the way around it. Actually, the house where Fiskdale lives is very small. So what else is there? There must be something, even after what Fiskdale says about selling off all the rooms, which is maybe true because he's a desperate man. But there's *something* there and we're going to find out what it is.'

'Which brings us back to the beginning. You said it was too dangerous.'

'Only if we get caught, and I've already done something to stop that.'

'Oh yeah?'

'After I saw there was something funny about the cupboard I came up with a plan to make it easy to return.'

'You're crazy.'

'You remember seeing the security system on the wall by the front door?'

'Not really.'

'Doesn't surprise me.'

'Shut up, Jonas.'

'Yeah whatever, Milly. Anyway, I thought if I stopped the security system from working we'd have a chance. You remember when I went to the loo, before we raided the sweetie cupboard?'

'Obviously.'

'Yeah, well, that was when I did it. I used my penknife to cut the wire. Just sliced it where it went down to the floor before entering the wall.'

'You did what?'

'So at the very least we've got to go back and fix it before Fiskdale finds out and smells a fish.'

'Smells a rat, Jonas. Smells a rat, not a fish.'

'Whatever, Milly. They're both equally smelly. So do you have a pair of old stockings we can use as masks to cover our heads? And while we're about it, one for Moses too.'

*

It's a funny thing. Any time I've ever done something I shouldn't have it was fun and exciting. And even more fun and exciting when I got caught. But this time I was just scared, scared like I'd never been scared before. Scared like I never knew what the word even meant before. I don't blame you if you're surprised I went along with Jonas' plan, because to be honest I was surprised I went along with Jonas' plan too. But I couldn't very well leave my little brother on his own to do what he was obviously going to do anyway. Especially when I got him into all this in the first place. You could say Jonas got us in deeper than we would have done, but actually that's a good thing. Somebody had to be the whistle blower for all the nasty, fishy, ratty things happening and I'm proud it's us. I really am.

We decided we couldn't waste time and had to return to Holbalm Hall ASAP. Luckily we both had after school groups next day, so one of us sneaked back to collect Moses while the other printed out an arial plan of Holbalm Hall in the ICT suite. I ended up doing the printing because Jonas also wanted to collect the soldering iron from the garage and enough sleeping tablets to stop Moses sniffing about the place after he'd done his bit. By giving him sleeping pills, that is, not using the soldering iron on him. The soldering iron was to mend the cut in the wire Jonas made with his penknife.

The three of us reunited at a point outside Holbalm Hall as far away from where Mr Fiskdale lived as possible. Everything was in place and our timing was good, only ten minutes gone since the school bell. Jonas had the bright idea of bringing in sweeties to trade for Dade Simpson's Grandad's taxi service and two taxis were waiting for us around the corner from the school gates. As part of the deal they had ladders to help us get over the wall.

'Weird,' I said, standing under a tree inside the grounds looking at the massive building before us, 'to think none of this is actually there.'

'I know,' said Jonas, pushing the ladder back over the wall. 'Isn't modern technology great? I just hope this works and our map isn't too out of date, because there could be anything here.'

He brought out a zip bag of sweeties and gave Moses a good sniff, then popped a few into his mouth with the promise of more to come.

'Now, boy,' he said, scratching Moses' head, 'this place is full of loads more sweeties like these. Whole cupboards full of good smells and tastes. I'm keeping you on the lead so you don't get too far ahead, but let's go find them.'

He gave Moses a final pat on the back and loosened his grip on the lead.

'Okay, boy, let's go. On y va. Vite, vite.'

Moses was off, racing in the direction of a large hedge in front of the main hall. He swiftly made his way round it, and then passed through walls and doors and windows like a dog with super powers.

'This is so cool,' said Jonas walking through the virtual house. 'I've got a video game like this, but I never thought I'd be doing it in real life. It'd be amazing to take my friends here.'

After ten minutes of passing through hallways with corridors and fireplaces and tapestries and pot plants and suits of armour we came out the other side and saw Mr Fiskdale's house across a lake.

'Right,' I said, 'after Moses' experience with the hedge I'm guessing that's real and I don't want to get wet. Let's go through the trees by the driveway over there.'

'Wasn't that fun, though,' said Jonas.

'Not if you were a burglar. There'd be nothing to steal.'

'True,' said Jonas, looking through a pair of binoculars. 'That's weird. Fiskdale must live in some sort of a gatehouse that's been disguised to look like a normal house. No sign of any secret room, though.'

Moses barked up a tree at a squirrel scampering out of his way, and started scraping at the bark with his paws.

'C'mon, boy,' said Jonas, pulling at the lead. 'Don't let us down now. We're almost there.'

Jonas released the lead after we got to the end of the driveway and Moses made a beeline for Mr Fiskdale's house. But the most amazing thing happened before he got there. Because just as Holbalm Hall turned out to be a building that wasn't actually there, so Jonas' secret room turned out to be an invisible building that *was* there. Moses yelped after squashing his nose against the outside wall.

'Good boy,' said Jonas, rushing up to give him a handful of Smarties, including enough sleeping pills to send him to the land of nod for several hours.

'Moses will be out of it soon,' he said, handing me the lead and feeling his way towards the building.

'Amazing, simply amazing,' he said after reaching it. 'You can actually feel the stone just like real stone, which I suppose it must be in a way. Now we've got to work out how to get in.'

I joined him at the wall and we split up and felt our way around the building in different directions, with poor Moses' lead wrapped around the branch of a nearby tree. After a few minutes Jonas waved his arm for me to come over.

'Okay, sis,' he whispered, pointing out an invisible window at the height of his shoulder, 'take a deep breath and look in there.'

Because I'm taller than Jonas it took me a little while to get the right angle for the window to appear, but after that I could see everything clearly. Inside was some sort of studio like you see on the telly with lights everywhere and big cameras on wheels. Over to one side Mr Fiskdale was holding a clipboard and talking into a phone and at the furthest end of the room a woman about Mum's age was arranging bits of furniture on a stage like the one we use for school plays and assemblies.

'Jonas,' I said, 'this is incredible. What do you think is going on? And how on earth has all this activity in there been made invisible?'

'I've no idea, sis, but I want to find out. Here, let me have another look.'

Jonas peered through the window for so long that I grew bored and began to regret coming along with him, especially since this weird room meant we'd probably never find a way through to all those sweeties now. Jonas didn't need me to hold his hand and there were a million better things I could be getting on with instead of watching him stare into space for ages. In fact, I had half a mind to climb one of the trees by the main wall and drop back over into reality, leaving Jonas to Moses and his crazy weirdo ideas.

Just then Jonas let out a terrible shriek and collapsed on the ground. The fall knocked him out and I didn't know what to do so I patted him about the face until he came round. He sat up and rubbed his eyes, unsure of where he was. Then he realised, rolled up into a ball and started crying harder than I'd ever seen him cry before.

I decided there was nothing I could do so I looked through the window to see what upset him so much. The stage was now organised for some kind of video shoot. I couldn't see clearly from the angle of the window, but it looked like an old tramp was sitting in a chair in the middle of the stage saying something into the camera about the bag of Knick-Knacks he was eating. He ate these Knick-Knacks very slowly and was exaggerating how much he enjoyed them. Surrounding him were giant advertising posters for Knick-Knacks, five different posters in different colours for different flavours.

Jonas tugged at my side before I was able to see any more. He was still snivelling, but had recovered from his fit. He held a finger up to his lips not to speak and pulled me down beside him.

'I don't know what to think anymore,' he said very quietly, 'but I'm scared, Milly. I'm really, really scared.'

'What on earth's the matter?' I said, irritated he was taking me away from what was going on through the window. 'Why are you acting so funny? You look like you've just seen a ghost.'

'That's because I have, Milly,' he said. 'That's because I have.'

7 Semi-beings

We almost got away with it. Okay, so Fiskdale might have suspected us of messing with his security system and wonder why, but because of this and our being careful not to leave any trace of our visit behind he had no proof we'd actually broken into Holbalm Hall. And strictly speaking we hadn't even broken in. We just climbed over a wall, gone through a building that wasn't there but looked like it was, peered through the window of another building that was there but looked like it wasn't, and climbed back over the wall again. No real harm done. But there was one person in all this we'd forgotten: Moses.

Look at it from Moses' point of view. He does all the hard work of getting us to our destination then falls asleep just when he's within tummy rumbling distance of his prize. So he does what any dog would: he goes back. He trots over to Holbalm Hall, barks at Fiskdale's front door until it opens, heads straight for the cupboard, paws it open and starts lifting packets of sweeties off the shelf with his snout. His return journey in the back of Fiskdale's car is much quicker. Dad's working, Mum's in the middle of cooking dinner and Jonas isn't allowed to answer the door, so I end up getting it.

'Hello again, Milly,' said Fiskdale, holding Moses under one arm and a doggy bag of sweets under the other.

'Oh, wow, hello,' I said, confused by how two totally different parts of my life could suddenly come together like this. One of these parts was really happy to see me and the other was not. To give you a clue, the happy one wagged his tail.

'Who is it?' Mum shouted from the kitchen.

'Nobody,' I shouted back.

'I think you and Jonas have got some explaining to do, Milly,' Fiskdale said.

'If it's nobody then how can you be talking to them?'

'Wait a minute please. Mum, it's obviously somebody, just nothing you need to worry about. And sometimes you can't just shut the door on people.'

'Is Jonas here too?'

'It's one thing shutting the door on people, darling, it's quite another entering into a conversation with them. Now who is it?'

'Yes, he is. Mum, it's nobody, but he's hard to get rid of.'

'How about we all go for a walk around the park together? I'll meet you and Jonas by the bandstand in ten minutes.'

'Hold on, darling, I'll be right there. Whoever this nobody is, they shouldn't be bothering my little girl.'

'Not possible, I'm afraid,' I lied. 'We're having dinner in ten minutes. Can't you smell the food cooking?'

'Just coming, darling.'

'You're a clever girl, Milly. I'm sure you can find a way. Incidentally, I think this is your dog. He has a keen interest in the contents of my cupboards for some reason. I can't think why. See you soon.'

I just managed to shut the door on Fiskdale when Mum came charging down the corridor, passing Moses on the way. I held the doggy bag out of view behind my back.

'It was just a man who found Moses and was returning him. He wanted a reward and I had to explain that we'd nothing to give him.'

'Good job, Milly. Really, some people have a cheek.'

*

By the time we arrive at the park we've got our version of events sorted. Fiskdale finds the security system damaged. He discovers Moses on the scent for sweeties, reads the address around his collar and puts two and two together. So we're greedy kids trying to take advantage of his generosity. So what. So we won't do it again. And that's about it. I feel we're in a strong position because Jonas still hasn't handed over his file, though he's not really been himself after seeing his ghost yesterday.

Fiskdale spots us and walks over to where we're sitting on a park bench by the bandstand overlooking the river.

'Milly, Jonas, here you are. I thought you'd be able to make it.'

He sits one bench along from us and looks over to the river. Something about him is different, like he's lost the power of his voice. I can't explain it, but we've got to listen very closely to hear what he's saying over the sound of the water.

'Pretend you don't know me. Just look like you are chatting amongst yourselves and I'll do the talking.'

Jonas giggles, in fear I think, and I elbow him in the ribs. He's been giggling like this all day, usually over silly, nothing things. Like I say, he's not really himself. And now I'm beginning to worry. Already Fiskdale has taken control. Already the meeting is turning out nothing like how I hoped.

'There are dark forces at work, which is why I wanted to meet you in a public place in broad daylight. Now clearly, judging from my impromptu canine visitor this afternoon, you think you can get involved in something you don't understand, something in fact that is too dangerous for you to understand. Let me make this clear to you then: whatever you are trying to do is putting your lives at risk.'

Jonas stops giggling and is now shaking violently.

'This will be the very last time we meet because I have a duty to your family to protect you and keep you safe from harm. I fear even meeting like this can have very serious consequences for us because these dark forces have knowledge of my work.

Jonas, it isn't your fault that you came across one of the semi-beings, as I call these apparitions. Just as it isn't your fault modern technology has enabled a memory system where semi-beings can feel trapped. Another time, another place and you'd be safe. But this is now and your life is in serious danger if you do not give me your semi-being ViM immediately. It's a terrible burden for me to carry but because I'm experienced in working with these forces I understand what they need to feel secure. But for you,' Fiskdale paused and glanced over to Jonas without smiling, 'there's no chance, I'm afraid.'

'Okay, okay,' stammered Jonas, shaking uncontrollably. 'We got into Holbalm Hall over the wall and used Moses to find our way around. It was the light that told me there was a secret room, the light coming into the cupboard. So we finally got to the room and I saw him. Saw him just as I see you sitting there on that bench now.'

'Saw who, Jonas?'

'The scary man on the beach in Indonesia.' Jonas looked directly at Fiskdale and spat out the words like he wanted rid of them forever. 'My ghost.'

'Aha,' said Fiskdale, smiling faintly. 'Well then.'

'You're right I don't understand. I don't think I'll ever understand. I've had nightmares for years, and a really bad one last night after I saw him again. I don't know why I used this memory to upload at the Memory Bank. I must have been crazy, but the category was adventure and it's the only real adventure I've ever had.'

'No need to worry any more, Jonas,' said Fiskdale. 'Simply hand over the file and you'll be safe.'

'But what's he doing here? How come he's travelled all this way? What does he want from me? What does he want to *do* to me?'

'Peace. He wants peace. This is the common thread I've discovered. These semi-beings are traumatised by an event of such power that it killed them and their families and the birds on the trees and even the trees themselves, wiped every living thing clear off the face of the earth for miles around. An event more traumatic than war or fire or plagues.'

'More traumatic than the Hydrogen bombs over Hiroshima and Nagasaki?' I said.

Perhaps this wasn't the best time to speak up, but we'd been studying Japan at school and I wanted to show Jonas wasn't the only member of the Buntly family who knew things.

'Even more traumatic than the bombs ending the Second World War, Milly.'

'I see. Wow.'

'Your experience, Jonas, is typical of many I've investigated. This is because the traumatic nature of how these semi-beings met their deaths leaves them in a permanent state of limbo between this world and the next. Whenever the volcano that killed them has any seismic activity they re-form out of the volcanic lava where they're locked for eternity and their spirits are free to wander. Krakatoa's been bubbling away now for six months. Consequently your semi-being has been about for six months, breathing oxygen and casting shadows just like the rest of us.'

'But Danemore's a long way from Krakatoa. What's he doing here?'

'Afraid I'm to blame for that. You see, I've become a little overenthusiastic in my work and have invited a number of these ghouls to come and stay for brief periods at Holbalm Hall. I've explained the nature of my work to them and they are usually only too happy to share experiences and talk about volcanoes. Because, after all, volcanoes are to blame for the state they're in.

Actually, they find their stay at Holbalm Hall a very positive one. First of all there are no volcanoes around here to bring back bad memories. And secondly they are able to meet fellow semi-beings. You know, share experiences about how they died and swap stories of what they get up to during periods of seismic activity. It can be quite a jolly time for them. Like a kind of support centre for ghosts.'

The mention of ghosts sets Jonas off again.

'What about my ghost?' he demanded. 'What do you know about him? For example, does he know I used him as an upload for an Adventure Memory?'

'Very good question, Jonas. Intelligent question too. Unfortunately this is where the dark forces come in and why you've got to watch your step. That is, until I have your file to work on so that I can neutralise the threat from this particular semi-being. Now tell me, do either of you know anything about the history of exploration amongst primitive tribes?'

I shook my head and looked to see if Jonas was doing the same, but he was shaking so much it was hard to tell.

'No? No reason you should, I suppose. Then you won't know the troubles early explorers had photographing these tribes. Because whenever a photograph was taken and it was shown to them there started to be a lot of problems. Why do you think this was?'

'I don't know,' I said. 'Because they didn't ask permission?'

'Much more serious than that, Milly. Because they thought the image they saw of themselves meant their soul had left them and entered the photograph. Basically, they thought the photograph robbed them of their soul. So they became very angry and there are many cases of these photographers ending up in the cooking pot as an ingredient for village stew.'

'Wow, that's really interesting,' I said. 'That's really cool. In a horrible kind of way. So what you're saying is these semi-beings, as you call them, are mostly from a time before photography was invented, let alone Memory Banks and ViMs.'

'Exactly, Milly. And their reaction to learning they've been used in this way has been unpredictable, but often extremely, wildly violent. Which is really the main reason I've taken the measure of coming to you to insist that Jonas hand over his ViM before any more time is lost, especially with this semi-being in the vicinity.

With the memory in hand, you see, I can explain to him that there is no harm and the action you have taken doesn't threaten him in any way. Otherwise, you'd better check the latest reports on Krakatoa's seismic activity or Jonas could come in for a nasty shock. You see, semi-beings need to be restlessly wandering at night time, something to do with them not really being proper living beings, and I can't vouch for Jonas' safety between sunset and sunrise.'

I was hoping to hear more about this, which was a much more interesting history lesson than the ones we get at school, but Fiskdale had stopped talking and was waiting for a response from Jonas. Many gallons of water must have passed down the river before he finally replied.

'Okay,' said Jonas slowly, 'I'll do it. I'll give you the thing. Do you think this means it'll be erased from my brain, so my nightmares stop too?'

'I couldn't tell you, I'm afraid, but at least it will make things less dangerous for you.'

'And will there still be the same reward?' I asked, keen to get back to the sweets. 'Do the terms of our agreement still hold?'

I have to admit it was touching to see Fiskdale looking relieved to be finally getting his hands on Jonas' memory, as much for the sake of Jonas' personal safety as his Vulcanology studies. It seems I'd got Fiskdale right all along and my little conspiracy theorist brother got him wrong. I won't let him forget this.

8 No Show

Everything about Fiskdale relaxed after Jonas agreed to hand over the file to him now instead of keeping to his original plan of waiting until he'd experienced similar ViMs at the Memory Bank. His mood changed as quickly as when a rainy sky brightens and the sun comes out. He was full of smiles and chatted away for so long I worried Jonas' semi-being might suddenly surge up out of the river and start doing terrible things to him like in some film. And maybe the only reason this didn't happen was that it wasn't dark yet, but at least Fiskdale was there to protect us if it did.

Back home, Jonas rushed to the computer to send his file over after dinner only to discover that it couldn't be done for some boring technical reason to do with being timed out. Fiskdale sounded narked when I explained this to him over the phone and that Jonas would try again tomorrow. He then made an arrangement for a car to pick us up after school to hand it over to him personally the next day.

'But we're due back ASAP tomorrow,' I said. 'We've not been home enough recently and Mum's getting suspicious. Plus they know there's no after school clubs or activities on.'

'How long does it take you to get back?'

'Twenty minutes if we don't miss the bus.'

'And if you do miss the bus?'

'That's never happened. Look, Mr Fiskdale,' I said, feeling bolder with him now, 'we're going to have to be home for 3:30 at the latest and there's nothing we can do about it.'

'Okay, Milly, then what I'll do is give you a guarantee that you and Jonas will be back in time. Deal?'

*

Jonas fretted all night about returning to the place where he'd seen his ghost. I could see the snag of being unable to send the file over to Fiskdale directly hit him hard. It didn't help the file had security software meaning it couldn't be opened for twelve hours after the failed attempt and he'd have to wait until 8:02 the next morning to put on disk. The school bus arrived at 8:13 and the stop was five minutes away, so he'd be really pushing it to get it done in time. Which was an added stress of course, kind of like stress doubled or squared.

'But that's the whole point of going round again ASAP,' I told him. 'So Fiskdale can fix your file and make sure you're out of trouble with your semi-being. It's your Get Out of Jail card.'

'Which is fine, yeah, except he hasn't got the file yet. The semi-being, what you and Fiskdale call him anyway, could jump out at any moment. Maybe he's hiding in the sweetie cupboard waiting for me. Maybe he knows I'm coming and he'll hijack the car on our way round, pretend he's a traffic warden or something.'

'Maybe, maybe, maybe. Jonas, you know who you sound like? Me when we found Fiskdale's business card in your capsule at the

Memory Bank. Aren't you glad I called him now? Can't you see he's trying to help us, just as he's trying to stop future volcanoes cause yet more devastation? Mr Fiskdale's our friend.'

'I suppose. But he's the reason I'm in trouble, don't you see, sis? I'd be a lot safer if he never invited my semi-being over here in the first place.'

'You don't know that. You don't know anything about semi-beings. You don't know the first thing about semi-beings and how they get about. They might be able to go through real buildings like we did at Holbalm Hall, float through walls as though they're not there. Look, what I'm saying is that if the semi-being thingy can come back to life out of molten lava then I don't think it'll have any problem tracking you down. The reason you're in trouble is because of that silly ViM of yours, not because of anything Fiskdale has done. And aren't we visiting during the day anyway, when he told us semi-beings only come out at night?'

'Suppose.'

He got his file off the hard drive and on to disk in time to catch the school bus after running all the way. Once he got his breath back I asked him where he put it. I was hoping it wasn't among the usual clutter of his school bag because there was no going back for another copy after he'd wiped the file from his hard drive. Unless he could upload the exact same memory twice, which I doubted, the disk he had on him now was the only copy in existence. He pretended to panic and search frantically through his bag before bringing an index finger up to his lips. He looked around the bus and lifted his shirt to reveal a money belt strapped to his waist. I was impressed. Jonas was thinking things through and leaving nothing to chance. My little brother was finally growing up.

Then he bottled it. The trouble started when I went to our usual meeting place after school to find him missing. Five slow minutes passed and he still hadn't turned up. Okay then. We both knew the car Fiskdale arranged for us would be waiting round the corner from the school. Maybe Jonas had gone there directly, and was sitting in it ready to go. Something we maybe should have discussed in advance, but I'd let him off this time. But he wasn't there. I tapped on the driver's side. After he rolled down his window I asked him if he'd seen Jonas. He stared blankly. I asked him if he'd seen a ten-year-old boy with red hair who spoke with a terrible French accent. Turns out this was along the lines of what he was going to ask me too. Jonas had gone AWOL.

I had to think quick and decided there was no point returning to Holbalm Hall without Jonas so I asked to be taken home.

'Sorry, love,' he said, 'I got my instructions. Wait here for Milly Buntly and Jonas Buntly and take them to 21 Random Avenue, Danemore via Holbalm Hall, Danemore.'

'The name's Alf, by the way,' he said, holding out his hand.

'Nice to meet you, Alf,' I said. 'I'm Milly Buntly. You know, the person you're supposed to pick up. 21 Random Avenue is where I live with Mum and Dad and my little brother Jonas, the other person you're supposed to pick up. So when I'm asking you to take me home I'm asking you to take me to 21 Random Avenue, which is the same 21 Random Avenue as the 21 Random Avenue you've got in your instructions to take me anyway.'

'No,' he said, scratching his head, 'there's something wrong here. There's something wrong in what you say. But I can't remember now what it is. Wait a minute. Let me get my work log from the glove compartment. Right, oh yes, I remember now. It says here: 'Two passengers to be collected from the southeast corner of Danemore Primary School'. So I've got the right address.'

He paused and looked out the taxi window.

'Now is this the southeast corner of Danemore Primary School? Not very clear that. Depends on how you look at it. Check the Sat Nav. Never Eat Shredded Wheat. Check. So I'm in the right place.'

We were making ground. Slowly, but we were making ground.

'Now it says here Milly Buntly is the name of one of the passengers and the name of the other passenger is Jonas Buntly. 'Milly Buntly and Jonas Buntly stop at Holbalm Hall on the way to 21 Random Avenue, where they get out, not later than 15:30', it says. Right. Thank goodness I've got that fixed in my mind. So, Milly, love, if that's who you say you are, where's this Jonas Buntly then?'

'Don't you see that's exactly why we're going home first?'

Another blank stare, more head scratching.

'Don't you see that's exactly why we are going to 21 Random Avenue first?'

'21 Random Avenue is where Milly and Jonas Buntly reach their destination and get out, no later than 15:30. That's right. But where's Jonas Buntly? And Milly and Jonas have to go somewhere first. Now where was that again?'

We were getting nowhere fast and wasting valuable time. Then I spotted two things that could maybe help persuade Alf to take me home. The logo on the side of the taxi identified it as one of Dade Simpson's granddad's cars. Now there was an odd thing about Dade Simpson's grandad that stuck in my mind from when we used his services to get to Holbalm Hall: he only liked to hire fellow grandads because he felt they were more trustworthy and put in longer hours than other folk. And the other thing I noticed was the holster by the steering wheel that had been especially designed for the flask of coffee Alf was using to refill his mug while he sat there getting muddled. So he's a grandad with a heavy caffeine habit. The coffee would play havoc with his Health Account. There wouldn't be many treats left over for the grandkids. And it just so happened we had plenty of kid's treats and coffee back home.

I went directly up to Jonas' room after settling with Alf and found him sitting on the floor in the middle of one of his silly games with AD. He didn't look like he was having a great time and sniffed loudly like he'd just been crying lots or was just about to cry lots or in between crying lots. He pretended I wasn't there and continued with his game, sniffing loudly and stopping every few minutes to blow his nose. There was nothing I could say that he didn't know himself, so I just stood there and waited. Jonas can play dumb like this for a very long time. Maybe this was his strategy for the situation with Fiskdale too. Ignore a problem long enough and it'll eventually go away. Unfortunately, in this case, I didn't think his problem would go away unless he did something about it first.

'Good move, AD,' he said to his invisible friend, as he moved a piece for him on the board. 'You've really got me this time, pal.' Before slamming one of his own pieces he'd hidden behind his back on the board. 'NOT!'

'Jonas,' I said softly and waited a few moments.

Nothing. Wait. Try again.

'Jonas, if you're not going to look at me you can at least hear me.'

No response.

'Were you too scared to go round?'

Nothing.

'I'll be there to protect you. Mr Fiskdale too. We'll both be there to make sure you're safe. Do you think I'd do something that would put my little brother in danger? Mum and Dad would never forgive me. It's just dropping the file off on the way home. No need even to get out of the car. And in daylight too, when Mr Fiskdale says semi-beings are sleeping.'

Jonas moves another of AD's pieces on the board. I decide to sit on the floor to be at eye level to him, careful to sit far away from AD in case I get accused of crowding him. This chat has got to be handled with the greatest delicacy, lots of nice soft big sister touches.

'Look, Jonas, I know it's scary for you. If I knew something out there was trying to get me I'd be a lot less brave than you are being right now. But I'd also do everything in my power to stop it and if that meant taking away whatever it was that caused the thing to feel this way, I'd do it. I'd do it in a flash.'

Jonas peeked out of the corner of his eye at me whilst fiddling with a counter as though considering AD's next move in the game.

'Especially if it helped other people like Amy feel better and Mr Fiskdale continue his research. Hopefully this will prevent other semi-beings from forming because areas around dangerous volcanoes will be evacuated before they erupt.'

I was beginning to run out of ideas.

'And we'll probably leave with enough sweeties to last us for years. We'll still be finding new places to hide them long after this business is forgotten about.'

'Yeah, sis, that's all you care about, isn't it?'

'What?'

'Sweeties is all you care about. You don't care about me or think about my feelings. You don't care if your little brother gets bludgeoned to death or stabbed or drowned. Killed in a hundred ways by something dead and scabby and out for revenge. You don't care.'

The problem now is he's using boy language and I'm not very good at boy language. Like, what does it mean to be bludgeoned to death? Is it like being tickled to death, or bored to death? Or maybe pecked to death, because a bludgeon sounds like a member of the pigeon family. Really, I didn't have a clue.

'That's not right, Jonas. What I want is for you to be safe and the best way to do this is for you to hand Mr Fiskdale the file he wants. You know, the one around your waist.'

'Correction. The one *was* around my waist.'

'What do you mean was? Where is it now?'

'Gone.'

'Gone? Gone where?'

'What does it matter, Milly?' said Jonas, sobbing and kicking the board over with his foot. 'Just gone alright.'

9 Strategies

'It's for you, Milly,' Mum shouted up to my room. It was just after nine o'clock that night. 'I'll put the phone down after you've picked up.'

'Hello, Milly.' It was Fiskdale.

'Who's that, Milly?' Mum said, still on the line. Drats and bums.

'Ah, is that Mrs Buntly?' Fiskdale said, his tone lightening and his voice changing. 'Excuse me for not introducing myself. I'm one of the other parents who helps out at Milly's dance class. Sorry about calling at this late hour, but you see Milly left her ballet shoes behind and I just wanted to let her know I've got them and will drop them off at reception on Monday.'

'Very good of you, Mister… I'm sorry. I didn't catch your name.'

'Mister Bones.'

'Unusual name. Is that with one bone or two? Two? I see. Very well then, Mister Bones.'

'Thank you. I was wondering where they were.' I tried not to giggle. 'Mister Bones.'

'Not like you to misplace things, Milly,' said Mum, with a hint of annoyance at being called up so late over such a trifling matter. 'Okay, putting the phone down now. I trust you won't be too long, Mister Bones. I don't know about you but it's nearing bedtime in this particular household.'

'Now,' said Fiskdale slowly, his tone darkening every second Mum was off the phone. 'Do you want to tell me all about what happened today?'

No, Mr Fishy Tail, I do not want to tell you all about what happened today. And I don't think you'll want to hear all about what happened today either. Because it will make you angry, even angrier than you are now, which is already pretty angry. You're scaring me, Mr Fish Head, and between semi-beings wandering about wanting to bludgeon my little brother, Jonas locking himself in his room and the file you want gone forever, the last thing I need is for you to be angry with me.

'Slight hitch.'

'We've just had one of those, Milly.'

'I know.'

Fiskdale sighed.

'So what's this one about?'

'Jonas missed the bus into school.'

'Did what?'

'Jonas didn't have time to copy the file on to disk.'

'Didn't do what?'

'Jonas got scared and went home on the bus after school.'

'Jonas did what?'

'Jonas is really sorry and thinks it's better if you come here for the file.'

'Thinks what? What? What? What?'

'Tomorrow afternoon before it gets dark. 3:30 at Random Avenue. Bring more sweets. See you then.'

I slammed the phone down and rushed over to Jonas' room.

'Okay, Jonas,' I shouted through the door, 'I just spoke with Fiskdale and saved you from almost certain bludgeoning. You can thank me later, but first we've got to get ready for our trip to the Memory Bank tomorrow.'

I put my ear to the door and heard soft sobbing under the duvet.

'So this is what you're going to do. Now listen carefully.'

*

It's Saturday morning and I'm totally stoked for Jonas. He totally nailed the new ViM. I know this because I interrogated him about it in the car on the way to the supermarket. I asked him detailed questions about the upload and checked his replies against the transcript of the original ViM. They're almost identical, but with a lot more fear and terror shown by Jonas the second time around, for obvious reasons. Jonas feels the only major difference is that seeing his semi-being at Holbalm Hall might have got jumbled up with his Krakatoa memories. Other than this he made only one change, which is no biggie and he doubts Fiskdale will even notice. He put the glass bead necklace of his favourite pop star round the semi-being's neck.

Everything was going well. Jonas was happy to have successfully uploaded ViM 2 and much calmer about being out in the daytime, now he'd finally got it into his head semi-beings only came out at night. I really felt we'd turned a corner and my little brother was coming back to me. And going to the supermarket is much more fun these days after Mum and Dad let us wander the aisles on our own. This usually means Jonas heading to the magazine racks by the entrance or hanging by the tank of fresh fish for sale, but today he went directly to the stationary section for a disk to copy his ViM on to and a sturdy envelope to put it in for collection.

As for me, I soon grew tired of looking at the same old products in the beauty section, and went over to the sweets to see how many of them are in our stash. Since the new laws came in sweets are kept in a controlled environment on shelving out of reach from children. You have to leave trolleys and baskets with the super-healthy consultant before entering and only one child at a time is allowed, so there's no chance of piggy backing your friends to get to your favourite sweet.

At the moment there's a heavy sales battle going on between the two industry leaders, the American giant Homemaker Industries and the European Delice-Stanley-Bahm group. I know this because Dad sometimes writes for the European lot for free and coined that really annoying phrase you see on posters everywhere:

Knick Knacks: Knever Knot Knice

Obviously, with Fiskdale being their UK representative, all the sweets in our stash are Homemaker Industries products. I'm not a big fan of American chocolate, but Homemaker Industries bought a small Belgian chocolatier last year and over half our stuff is from there, with the rest made up of crisps, dips, candies, lollies and sticks, snout fillers, snack stoppers and thirds ways. Both sides of the aisle are covered with posters and banners encouraging you to go for one lot of products over another.

At the bottom of the aisle there's a dead end designed to stop through traffic and help the super-healthy consultant monitor activity. Usually there's nothing but stock overflow here, but a taste comparison counter with someone dressed up like a giant Y-not is on today. The outfit was made out of a sponge-like material the same colour as the packets on the table, with the Y's two arms coming out of the character's head like he's an alien from outer space.

I never turn down an opportunity to get something for free, so I go over. The taste comparison is between Y-nots and Knick-Knacks. I try both thinking they'll taste similar, but they don't. Knick-Knacks have the classic flavour and slinky smooth slide down the throat feel that makes you want to have another one immediately. And Y-nots don't. I mean, they're okay, but they're not even in the same league as Knick-Knacks. The makers know this and don't waste time telling you anything different. Instead, there's a fact sheet with bright graphs and bar charts showing that Y-nots have 50% fewer calories and only 0.5 grammes of fat per chip compared with 2 grammes of fat per chip for Knick-Knacks.

I feel sorry for the person standing in this sad costume having to promote Y-nots. Everybody loves Knick-Knacks and nobody's ever heard of Y-nots, let alone thought about choosing them as a healthy alternative. Everybody likes Knick-Knacks because they're full of fat and everybody likes fat. If there was a sweet made up of all the different fats you could get in the world it would be the most popular sweet ever, so long as you called it Spring Snack or Harvest Crunch, and not Fat Bar.

'I mean, I like these Y-nots all right,' I said to the Y-not character, taking a third handful from the bowl, 'but c'mon, who doesn't love a packet of Knick-Knacks? So Homemaker Industries wins again.'

'That's where you're wrong,' Y-not said. 'We know Knick-Knacks is the established marketplace leader, but people worry about their fat per chip content. People are more aware of these things in our health conscious times. And we think new legislation will come in soon calculating the fat content of individual shopping baskets to charge the shopper's Health Account. Which is why Homemaker Industries is proud to have launched the Y-not, a healthier, lighter alternative to the Knick-Knack.'

'What, you mean Homemaker Industries don't make Knick-Knacks?'

Duh, of course not, or Dad wouldn't be making up silly catchphrases for them. I must have forgotten and thought they were a Homemaker Industries product because an advert for Knick-Knacks was being made in the Secret Room at Holbalm Hall. At least that's what I thought was happening. But why would Fiskdale be making an advert for their biggest rivals?

I was thinking about this heading back to Mum and Dad when I got stuck in Frozen Foods. A woman was taking ages to decide between two economy packets of peas and had left the freezer door wide open, completely blocking the way for other trolleys. Then as soon as she closed the door a trolley pushed through when I had clear right of way. I know these things aren't set in stone because The Aisleway Code for Supermarket Trolleys isn't out yet, but I'd been waiting a lot longer and this trolley hadn't even fully come to a stop before it was off again. I looked up to give the trolley user a piece of my mind and saw a face that gave me such a shock I ditched my trolley and ran to find Jonas immediately.

'Jonas,' I said, 'you're not going to believe this but I just saw your semi-being from the Secret Room. He's in Frozen Foods. Come on, or you'll miss him.'

'Oh yeah, and what was he doing? Don't tell me. Buying oven cook chips, family size Pizzas and big tubs of Haagen Dazs to fill the semi-beings up for all that night wandering they have to do.'

I had to laugh.

'You see, they can have blowouts like this every night because they don't have Health Accounts. And why's this? Oh, I forgot. Because they're actually dead, that's why. C'mon, sis, pull the other one.'

'Fine. Come along if you don't believe me.'

We found the semi-being in Wine, scanning for special offers. Judging by the two bottles in his shopping trolley, he was going for the three for two offer on selected wines and struggling to find a third that would make the deal sweet so he'd feel good about buying three times more wine than he actually wanted. I've been there myself, though not with wine of course, so I know how it feels.

'Okay, so now he's getting some booze for a party. After all, it can't be much fun being the living dead. C'mon, Milly, let's get back to Mum and Dad.'

It was interesting, though, and I was disappointed Jonas didn't want to stick around for longer. Then I remembered it was only me who'd seen the semi-being out of his robe at Holbalm Hall, so for Jonas he was just a regular shopper. After all, as little as we knew about semi-beings, it was for sure they weren't spending their non-wandering time browsing three for two offers at the local supermarket. Still, it set me thinking and I kept my eye on him. He came out of the store just in front of us and was parked a few cars down, so at least I was able to take a note of the licence plate before he drove away.

*

The more I thought about it, the more my experiences at the supermarket didn't add up. Either that, or what I thought I saw through the window of the Secret Room wasn't what I actually saw and the mystery shopper was a different person from Jonas' semi-being entirely. One thing was certain, though. We had to do more research, and there was a more immediate issue to be dealt with first.

'So, Jonas,' I said, 'you're all set. You've got the ViM on disk all ready for collection.'

This was in the living room where Mum and Dad could come through at any time, so I wasn't surprised Jonas ignored me. I knew the answer anyway because Jonas spent the last half hour on his computer upstairs and looked very calm when he came down and switched on the TV to play a fighting game, with the jiffy bag resting on top of the console. Now he was into his game he'd no time for anything else. It was perfect for what I needed to do.

'Did you buy two envelopes, by the way? In case you made a mistake with the address or something.'

He'd just got through to the end of the stage he was at and a screen came up to give him options to save or continue.

'Yeah, got two of everything,' he said, flinging the jiffy bag over. 'Two card backed envelopes, two jiffy bags.'

'Very good,' I said, getting up. 'Hold on. I'll be back in a minute.'

I looked round to see if Jonas noticed I was on my way upstairs with the parcel, but he'd already clicked to continue and was back in the game. Perfect.

It didn't take me long to get into Jonas' Memory Bank account now that he'd given me the password and pop a fresh disk (he'd bought two of these as well) into the drive to make a copy of a different ViM. But it was just as I feared. There was security software for copying files meaning I couldn't perform the same function again for another 47 minutes, when it would be too late. No matter, I'd just use one of my own. We could still say the disks got mixed up.

The courier arrived at 3:30 on the dot. The parcel he delivered was addressed to me and contained a pair of ballet shoes several sizes too big, together with some sweets as a token of apology from Mr Bones for holding on to them for so long. Jonas was so keen to hand the file over to the courier he ignored our pre-arranged plan and pushed the bag into his gloved hands before he'd even got off his bike.

'You're supposed to wait until the end to give him the parcel,' I said, after the bike zoomed off.

'Sorry, sis,' he said. 'I just couldn't wait to have this over and done with. To have this nightmare over forever.'

He looked so happy and relaxed. Fixing a snack from the fridge, lining up a few Slam bottles, hunkering down for a long gaming session. The very picture of the carefree little boy from before this all started. I must admit I did feel the teeniest bit guilty.

1O Toothpaste Ninja

Adrian Gulp was an actor, the last of the famous Gulp acting dynasty. I had to look up what dynasty meant. Basically, it's something that goes on for ages and ages. Theodus Gulp was very big in the Edwardian era. It's known as the Edwardian era because a King called Edward was on the throne. Now, you'd think the time his daughter Emma Gulp was a movie star would be called the Elizabethan era because a Queen called Elizabeth was on the throne. But you'd be wrong. It's actually called the Sixties. The Elizabethan era was hundreds of years before when another Queen called Elizabeth was on the throne. This is very confusing and something I hope future historians fix.

Adrian Gulp is Emma Gulp's son with Richie Fellows. Richie Fellows was also an actor, but not as successful as Emma Gulp. So poor Adrian had no real choice about what he was going to do in life. Only he wasn't very good at it. He lost his Equity Card, which is like a passport to act, in 2010. This was due to an onstage fistfight with one of the other dwarves during a Christmas run of Snow White. He might have got away with it only the performance was in front of a ward of sick children. Since then he's struggled to make ends meet. So it stands to reason he's teamed up with Fiskdale, another desperate man. I mean, just look at his clothes. The reason I recognised him so easily when we met in the supermarket was because he was in the same tramp clothes he wore in the Secret Room. Recent CCTV footage of him online always shows him in these clothes. This must be what happens when you spend more time in Wine than Beauty.

All this took about twenty minutes to find out. I used the license plate from his car to get a name and address. You didn't used to be able to do this, but new rules last year introduced an openness policy for insurance claims in case another vehicle hits yours. The license plate together with the name, address and bank details of the vehicle owner instantly appears on your Sat Nav so everything can be managed without having to get out and exchange numbers. So it follows you can find a car owner's registration details by typing the license plate into a database. And once you've got that you can find out practically everything you've ever wanted to know about them online.

This is why most teachers at my school buy private license plates that can't be traced. It's expensive, but worthwhile in case the deepest, darkest secrets from their past return to haunt them. For instance, a supply teacher took over Miss Humphrey's P5 class for two weeks when she was ill last year, and rolled up in an old banger with state license plates. The following morning he came into class to find the whiteboard covered with photos from his days as an underwear and swimwear model beneath a banner reading, 'Turnip strips off'. Mr Tipurn (called 'turnip' as a boy because of his red face) confiscated 43 pairs of pants and 17 swimsuits over the next three days and didn't return for the second week Miss Humphrey was off.

But I'm getting away from my story. So Adrian Gulp's an actor and I reckon he played the role of Jonas' semi-being in the Secret Room. This could have been for many reasons. First of all, I reckon the chances of semi-beings speaking English are almost zero because when you think about it there aren't many volcanoes in places where people speak English. I mean, there's the San Andreas Fault in the US, but that's only produced earthquakes like the one that hit San Francisco in 1906 and it doesn't sound like earthquakes cause semi-beings. From what Fiskdale said, it's active volcanoes re-erupting that bring them out, and I never heard of an earthquake hitting the same place twice. And Adrian Gulp was definitely in tan make up for his role in the Secret Room to make him look like he was from a hot country.

I had no idea why Gulp was filmed munching Knick-Knacks, though. Nor why he promoted a Delice-Stanley-Bahm product when Fiskdale worked for their biggest rivals. So that was one thing to find out. Another thing to find out was whether the semi-being Jonas saw in the Secret Room was just Adrian Gulp got up in a cape. I thought if Jonas could get proof of this then he might start to feel a little better about things and not be so scared when I broke it to him that I sent Fiskdale the wrong ViM.

The difficulty then was that I couldn't be certain the actor playing his semi-being would be doing all the wandering about Fiskdale told us semi-beings got up to after dark. That is, if semi-beings did actually exist. The more I learned about Fiskdale the more I agreed with Jonas' that he lied about everything, but putting Jonas in danger with a crazy wandering semi-being out for his guts on the off chance he was played by an actor was a pretty big risk. If only there was a way I could be surer about the identity of the wandering semi-being. What about Jonas' pop star's glass bead necklace? If the wandering semi-being wore this, then he wasn't genuine. Drats and bums, then I remembered. I never sent Jonas' semi-being ViM over to Fiskdale after all.

Okay, back to square one. Look through the transcript of Jonas' ViM I sent over to Fiskdale. All it says is that the semi-being is 'dressed like a monk'. It didn't matter if there was any extra information about the semi-being's appearance in Jonas' ViM because Fiskdale didn't have access to it. I asked Jonas what his semi-being looked like when he saw him again in the Secret Room. He said he looked exactly the same as the figure he'd seen on the beach in Indonesia. How? He wore the same hood and walked in the same slow way. What about his face? He didn't see his face, just like he hadn't seen it on the beach. He paused his game for a moment to think about this.

'Maybe it doesn't have a face. Maybe it lost its face in the volcano. It melted off in the heat or something so it wears the hood not to upset people.'

'How could you tell it was your semi-being then?'

'It was just a feeling in my tummy, really. You know, like you're going to be sick.'

It was just a feeling. Duh, so basically you could put Dad in a cape and tell him to walk in a funny way and you've got Jonas' semi-being. My poor simple little brother, this changes everything. And there's only one way of being absolutely sure. Call Fiskdale's bluff and get him to bring out Jonas' semi-being for some bludgeoning. Which shouldn't be too difficult because he hasn't received the ViM yet. He must have lost patience and realised the carrot of using the ViM to help the semi-being wasn't working and it was time to bring out the stick.

In other words, we didn't have to do anything but sit tight and wait for Fiskdale to make his move. And the longer we sat put the more likely he was to make the move we wanted. Excellent. Of course, the difficulty now was to persuade Jonas of this after giving him the bad news his ViM hadn't gone over to Fiskdale after all.

But things moved too quickly for that. First of all there was no contact from Fiskdale after he received the disk with the wrong ViM, though it might have taken him a little while to realise this. After copying it on to his computer he'd have rushed down to the Memory Bank to download it from his account. I wasn't sure whether you could just roll up and use capsules in this way, though. He'd probably have to queue in the line of no-life saddos hoping someone misses their turn and they get an extra go. Users are only allowed one session per week, with the exception of pensioners and the unemployed, who get two because they have more time on their hands. I'm not even sure about this, though, because Granny always seems to be going. There are special Revival Memory categories for OAPs. You can choose between Fifties, Sixties and Seventies Memories. Or the first half of the Elizabethan age, as it should be called, though I can see how using the name of the decade is better in this case. Maybe it'll take another hundred years for it to be called the Elizabethan age so the Noughties, Tens, Twenties, etc., can be used to categorise our Revival Memories when we're old.

I was sitting on my bedroom windowsill thinking these thoughts, looking out over the street in case Jonas' semi-being turned up. When there it was. It must have turned suddenly into our street because it was already very close and I'd been scanning all the different access points for over an hour. There it was: a hooded, ghostly figure slowly approaching our house. I understood now what Jonas meant about not seeing the face, because the figure's head was bent down so low there was no way of doing this unless you were on the ground directly below.

My stomach churned and I felt funny in the head, like it was filling with smoke. I couldn't think and felt sick. Just like Jonas said. The figure approached our front gate. Hold on, there was a pillar between my window and the gate. How did I know this? I felt sicker. The information was inside my gut. I retched. I retched again and climbed down from the windowsill. The figure was now inside the gate. I ran to Jonas' room. The figure paused. Jonas was playing his fighting game. He ignored me. I sat on the floor holding my stomach. Time passed. I retched again. The figure paused. Jonas ignored me. I crawled towards him. He turned round, opening his mouth to speak. From the facts I pieced together later it must have only been minutes after I entered the room, but it felt like hours.

'Milly,' he said, 'what are you doing here?'

Before shouting at me to get out and returning to his game.

Five minutes pass. I give up trying to crawl. I retch once, twice, three times. Jonas humphs and saves the game. He switches off his computer and complains about me to AD. He comes over and I retch again. He worries about sick landing on his French flag rug. Then he sees the state I'm in.

'Zut alors,' he says. 'Zut alors!'

He asks if I'm all right. He kneels down beside me and grabs my hair and scrapes it clear of my eyes. He looks at me carefully. He lifts me up by my arms and hauls me to the bathroom. I vomit in the toilet. My mind clears.

'Your ViM,' I splutter through saliva. 'You know, your semi-being thingamajig.'

He holds my hair up, wipes vomit from my chin with toilet paper.

'It's here, outside now. Outside the door now.'

Jonas continues wiping.

'Jonas, your ViM is inside the gate right now.'

Jonas drops the sick covered toilet paper. He stands to his full height, his body pumped with adrenalin from the game he's playing.

'Right,' he says quietly.

'Right,' he says, more loudly.

He picks up Mum's electric toothbrush.

'Right,' he says, steeling himself.

He selects Dad's deodorant spray from the bathroom cabinet. He holds the spray and toothbrush as though they're weapons and looks in the mirror. He puts them down, squeezes out some toothpaste and applies it like war paint on his cheeks and arms. He puts Mum's shower cap over his hair and opens his mouth to produce the most horrible noise I've ever heard. He rearms himself, switching the toothbrush on and spraying great circles in the air with the aerosol can. He takes a deep breath, screams loudly, kicks the bathroom door open and runs down the stairs out into the front garden.

I still feel sick and keep my head over the toilet bowl. When not retching I listen out for what's going on downstairs.

I can hear Dad shout in the hallway, then Mum. She shouts Dad's name and then Jonas' name, then Dad's name again and Jonas' name again. She has a loud voice. Out in the street there's a lot of screaming and yelling, followed by the sound of a scuffle and shouting and arguing and pleading. Jonas and Mum and Dad's voices are all distinct, joined by what sounds like an older male voice.

In the distance a man asks loudly if they know what time it is and the noise crosses the front door and enters the house. First it's in the corridor and then it's in the living room, where it dies down. Peace returns to the house and I must have nodded off because the next thing I know I'm woken up by a much closer noise. I prop myself up and look around. Dad is standing in the doorway, a monk's cape draped over his left arm.

11 Let Off

'You'd better come downstairs,' Dad said.

It takes me a little while to come round and I struggle to lift myself up from the bathroom floor. Usually Dad would help me but he just stands there. He waits for me to go through the doorway into the corridor. My head hurts and I don't know what to think.

Dad joins me at the top of the stairs.

'Oh Milly, Milly, Milly,' he says, 'what have you done? You're grounded. For a long time, I think.'

Nothing unusual there, but I feel sad to see he's been crying. I have a good relationship with Dad where I can say anything to him and he'll give me a straight answer. Now when I need him the most this isn't possible. Things have gone too far. Jonas and me had been playing in the adult world for too long.

My only hope was that what I'd find in the sitting room was a small thing. Sometimes big things for children are small things for adults. Hopefully this was one of these times. My mind was racing too hard to form any clear ideas. All I could think about was how much Mum and Dad would feel let down.

The living room smelt strongly of extra mint toothpaste. In fact, there was toothpaste all over. Toothpaste all over Jonas obviously, but also all over Mum who was holding Jonas, all over the sofa where they were sitting and all over Adrian Gulp, who was in the armchair opposite them. In fact, there didn't seem to be anywhere to sit that wasn't covered in toothpaste. I stood by the window overlooking the street and Dad sat next to Jonas on the sofa. He didn't seem to mind the toothpaste and then I realised it was all over him too.

Mum spoke first.

'Jonas, do you have anything to say to your sister?'

Everybody looked at Jonas, who was bent forward on his knees with his head in his hands. He was sobbing quietly and redder than I'd ever seen him before. He didn't reply.

'All right, then,' Mum continued. 'I'll do the talking then, shall I?'

Nobody made an effort to stop her. I noticed Adrian Gulp, whose face was covered in shoe polish as well as toothpaste, was wearing his usual tramp clothes. He didn't look any happier than anyone else.

'We've been worrying about Jonas for a while. He's not finishing what's on his plate, coming and going at odd hours and acting jumpy around the house. None of this is normal behaviour and now we know the responsibility for it lies with you. Is there anything you want to tell us about what you've been doing with Mr Gulp?'

Adrian Gulp coughed and cleared his throat. He looked even older and less healthy than he did at the supermarket.

'They know everything I'm afraid, Milly. I told you this was a bad idea. I'm very ashamed, but what can a poor old soak do?'

'Well exactly, Mr Gulp,' Mum said without taking her eyes off me. 'Which leads us to the question of how you were expecting to pay for it, Milly. Because Mr Gulp here would want something for every time he put his silly cape on, and alcohol supplies here are limited. We're clearly giving you too much pocket money. Well, that's one of the things going to change around here. Isn't it, Desmond?'

'What were you thinking?' said Dad, rubbing Jonas' back. 'To steal my best bottle of whisky.'

'I hate you, Milly,' said Jonas.

'Well,' I said, and left a long pause to be filled by Jonas or Adrian Gulp, or anyone for that matter.

'Well. Obviously I'm sorry and accept whatever punishment you give me.'

'And Jonas,' Dad said.

'Sorry, Jonas. I'm really sorry okay.'

Now could somebody please tell me what's going on?

'I mean,' Mum said, 'how could you even come up with the idea? It's just such a, such a...'

'An evil idea,' said Dad. 'That's what it is. An evil idea.'

'Well,' I said.

Finally Adrian Gulp spoke up.

'To be fair to your daughter, Mr Buntly, I don't think her intention was evil. The idea was just to give Jonas a little shock. It was meant as a kind of joke, because after all, who really believes in ghosts?'

'That's right,' I said, catching on, 'it wasn't meant seriously. And Mr Gulp was going to reveal himself at the end to show Jonas that his fears were all in his head. It was to help Jonas stand up to his fears really.'

'And in the meantime, you had Jonas so out of his wits with fear that he runs through the house covered in toothpaste and attacks Mr Gulp with toiletries. This, Milly, is not a boy playing one of your silly games. This is a boy scared out of his wits. A boy in fear of his life.'

'Yes,' said Adrian Gulp, 'the toothbrush was really quite painful. And the aerosol is still stinging my eyes. You should have warned me Jonas was quite the little terror when he gets going.'

'Sorry,' I said.

'Okay,' Mum said to Adrian Gulp, 'we won't press charges because this would drag our children through the courts and that's the last thing we want. I think we should draw a line under this whole sorry episode. You are free to go. Your wonderful mother will be turning in her grave that you have stooped so low at the age most men are putting up their feet and joining amateur painting classes. Shame on you.'

Adrian Gulp rose from his seat and hauled his tramp trousers up around his waist.

'I hope you can find it in yourself to forgive us, Jonas. But at least you know there's no spook chasing you. Mr Buntly, Mrs Buntly, thank you for being so understanding. Adieu.'

'No, wait,' I shouted as our chief witness walked out the door. 'Let me talk to him a minute.'

'You're not going anywhere I'm afraid, Milly,' said Mum.

'But I just want to say something to him.'

'Out of the question,' said Dad. 'You've got a lot of making up to do to your brother and it's starting now.'

I had no option but to watch Adrian Gulp slip away from under our eyes. Drats and bums.

*

Naturally it wasn't in either Jonas' or Adrian Gulp's interest to tell Mum and Dad the truth about what they were up to. In fact the story they somehow managed to cobble together had only one victim in it: me. I was facing a future of household chores, no sweets or pocket money, no after school clubs, no dance lessons, no visiting friends, no Memory Bank trips and straight home after school every day until at least the school holidays, which were still well over a month away. The one place I was allowed to go was to Jonas' room to see if he had any jobs that needed doing.

'That was fun,' said Jonas after letting me in when things calmed down.

'You were amazing,' I said.

'It was just like one of my fighting games.'

'You were so brave. Jonas the street fighter, Jonas the toothpaste ninja, Jonas my hero.'

'Yeah well, I was a little scared to be honest. I didn't know what I'd find, if it was a real semi-being or not. Especially after you saw him and were sick like that.'

'The way you ran down the stairs when I told you it was outside.'

'I was just angry Fiskdale hadn't fixed things like he said he would after I gave him the ViM.'

'Actually, Jonas, about that ViM.'

'And I was pumped up after bashing Torr the Terrible and getting through to face Inga the Incredible. Because if you get to fight Inga then you're a good fighter. Tim Trott says he's beaten Inga and boasts about it all the time but nobody has seen the footage so if I beat Inga and make a record of it then I'll be the first in Year 5.'

'Right. Jonas, about that ViM.'

'I went at him with a straight attack on his legs. He went down and then it was time to use my weapons. I could see he was just some old drunk in a cape but he was trying to unscrew this bottle so I sprayed deodorant in his face and stuck the toothbrush up his nose.'

'Excellent. So how did you come up with what to say to Mum and Dad?'

'It was the tramp. What's his name again?'

'I think Mum called him Mr Gulp.'

'Right, Mr Gulp. Well he just said you got him to do it. He used you instead of Fiskdale. Quite clever really.'

'So he was covering up for his boss.'

'Covering for Fiskdale, right. Which is hard luck on you, sis.'

'I can't believe Mum and Dad fell for that. They must think I'm really weird.'

'Well, they knew I was having nightmares ever since Indonesia. And they knew I recently made a ViM out of it so it was still on my mind a lot.'

'But to actually go as far as to get somebody to pretend to be a ghost and scare you.'

'But that's what you're like, Milly. You're always scheming and trying to get the better of people.'

'S'pose.'

'Mum was very angry and Dad was disappointed. He actually cried when the tramp, Mr Gulp, told him about how you did a search for local actors and offered him alcohol from Mum and Dad's secret stash in exchange for dressing up and doing some haunting.'

'That's unfair. I'd never do that.'

'Yeah, well it just made the tramp's story more real when you saw the state he was in.'

'S'pose.'

'That was the bit where I helped him out. I said I'd seen him the day before in our street and was really scared and ran to you and you just laughed at me.'

'What.'

'That's right. You told me I was a fool and that ghosts didn't exist. That was when Dad got up and started doing circles round the room.'

'And then what happened?'

'Well, the tramp told us he met you after school. You know, the time we went out to see Fiskdale at the park and Mum and Dad wondered where we were.'

'Very clever. So Fiskdale must have told Gulp about this meeting in case you didn't send the ViM over and he had to go and do a little haunting.'

'I guess. Anyway, that was the point Dad stormed out the room to get you. The tramp told them you brought a bottle of Dad's favourite whisky. He must have seen the bottles in the drinks cabinet in the corner. Since then, after things quietened down, I went and poured the whisky down the sink and hid the bottle in my room.'

'Great. So now I'm a thief as well. Great work, Jonas.'

'And that's the story really. I thought the tramp was clever to come up with all that stuff off the top of his head. I don't think we'll be seeing him again.'

'No. I don't think we will either.'

Jonas got up and opened the door.

'So that's that then. Anyway, sis, you've probably got lots of chores to be doing and I want to get back to preparing my fight with Inga. See you later.'

*

Amazing. The whole thing was amazing. How Mum and Dad could believe all those horrid stories about me. How Jonas could rush outside and tackle what could have been a dangerous semi-being to the ground. How Adrian Gulp could be so convincing about total nonsense. And finally, how unpleasant my life was going to be over the next few weeks.

There's still lots to do though. We'd made good progress in uncovering Gulp and discovering he played the semi-being in the Secret Room. I don't really know what this means yet, but it's a good first base to reach and one that marks the end of the line for Jonas. He's too little to go any further and I didn't want to ruin his moment of glory by telling him the truth about his ViM. At least there'd be no more trouble with semi-beings wandering about wanting to bludgeon him. And Jonas had himself to thank for that. I never knew he could be so brave, but the adventure was over for him.

I was just sorry I never had a chance to speak to Gulp on my own. It would have saved time to ask him a few questions and find out exactly what was going on in the Secret Room. I didn't think he'd be so easy to trace now. Either he'd report back to Fiskdale and keep out of sight or he'd go on the hoof and leave Danemore forever. I figured my next move anyway, one I could do on my own. The important thing was to find out the identity of the other character I saw Gulp playing in the Secret Room. And to do this I needed to see the ViM he featured in.

12 Santa Tramp

Things quietened down after the great toothpaste skirmish, and Jonas was happier than ever. As well as uncovering the mystery of his semi-being, he beat Inga the Incredible and moved on to Vladimir the Vanquisher. All his free time was taken up preparing for this match. He swapped notes with fighters who'd faced Vladimir in the past, worked on his strategy and looked up cheats online. Dad finished a big writing commission and spent most of the time watching the World Cup just started on Super HD. Even Moses took a breather from all that digging and exploring, giving Mum a chance to make a new toy for Baby Ellen. And what of Fiskdale? Well, things went quiet on that front too.

In fact, the only one doing any real work around here is yours truly. I've never worked so hard, washing, scrubbing and cleaning all day long to pay off my forfeit. Part of the forfeit is to wait on Jonas, which basically means feeding him a constant supply of Slam bottles, so there will be more work for me at the Recycling Centre as well. And in the evenings I've been recording this story on to disk. I was hoping I could do some Memory Bank magic and it'd record by itself, but I've had to tell the whole thing the old fashioned way, via a microphone on the side of the computer. This takes ages and my main reason for working hard during the day is to give myself enough time to record at night. The other reason is so Mum and Dad see all the hard work I've put in and let me go to the Memory Bank with them after recycling as a treat for good behaviour.

So what do you think I should do next? Should I sit and wait for Fiskdale to get in touch, or contact him first? I mean, I already know what I want to say, but the problem is my movements are restricted. When Fiskdale finds this out it might put him off, or more likely he'll find a way to take advantage of the situation.

Anyway, six days have passed since Jonas tackled Adrian Gulp, it's almost two weeks since we found the business card, I'm up to date with my record of events and it looks like Mum and Dad will let me join them at the Memory Bank tomorrow. The last point is the most important because I reckon all dealings with Fiskdale can be managed there so that he never realises I've been grounded. As such it's probably best to call him now rather than have him call me whenever he wants. Plus these have been six long days and I'm really bad at waiting for things.

So here goes, after dinner on Friday. Clear the throat and keep calm, dial the number and wait. A voice familiar to millions comes on the line.

'Hello. Thomas Fiskdale speaking.'

'How are you, Mr Fiskdale?'

'How do you think I am, Milly?'

'I have no idea.' Cool and calm now Milly, cool and calm. 'But I do know we have something you want.'

'Yes, you do.'

Fiskdale sounded tired, whether with life itself or just me it was hard to say.

'Yes, I'm sorry about that. But I've got the disk here on me now and I was thinking I could maybe drop it off at the Memory Bank tomorrow.'

'That would be fine, Milly. How can I be sure I'll get it this time though?'

Which was a reasonable question and one I'd already considered, since I really did want to give Fiskdale Jonas' ViM this time. After all, he'd made his move so now it was my turn to mix things up and see what came out of it.

'I'll leave it at reception or any other place you'd like. I know you have a friend working there called Giles and I could always give it to him.'

'Giles,' he said, sounding alarmed. 'How do you know about Giles?'

'Don't you remember? You mentioned him once, right at the beginning when I first got in touch. Anyway, it makes sense you know somebody working there. How else would you know which capsule to put your card in for Jonas to find, and at what time, because these capsules have a quick turnaround between users.'

'I see. Very clever of you, Milly.'

'Right then. I'm glad you agree.'

Pause and count to five.

'Oh, I almost forgot. There is one tiny thing you can do for me in return.'

Fiskdale let out a deep sigh.

'What's that, Milly?'

'For some reason Jonas is very upset by your story of semi-beings. If you could let him see another ViM with one in it I think it would really settle his nerves. So if you set this up for him tomorrow…'

'I can't possibly do that,' Fiskdale interrupted. 'These things are like horror films. I just don't think it's wise to expose them to boys of Jonas' age.'

'I'm sorry to hear that.'

I expected some such guff and had an answer all ready.

'By the way, Mr Fiskdale, talking about films, have you seen any Adrian Gulp movies recently?'

*

It all worked out better than I expected. My main concern after getting Fiskdale to let Jonas see one of his ViMs was that he'd choose the ViM himself. After all, I couldn't very well say I wanted the one with the tramp in it because then he might realise I'd seen the advert for Knick-Knacks being made in the Secret Room. But as luck would have it Fiskdale was so worried about the effect these ViMs would have on Jonas that he set up a special screen menu giving the name and advisory age of the entire lot with a guarantee from me that Jonas would only select one with a PG rating. I have to say I was actually quite touched by this. It showed Fiskdale cared. It would have worked too, because Jonas is a very law abiding citizen who's never knowingly watched anything above a PG in his life. He's kind of square that way.

Only it wasn't Jonas who watched the ViM, of course. It was me. I'd buttered Jonas up for a capsule swap with some record breaking Slam deliveries. Each bottle of Slam arrived super quick and cooled to his preferred temperature with the cap unscrewed and a straw bobbing in it, enabling him to refill and continue gaming without pause. Then I chose a moment in the game that looked like it needed intense concentration to ask him about swapping capsules so he'd say yes without thinking just to get me off his back.

So Saturday arrives and I slide into Jonas' capsule and face a menu listing seventeen different ViMs, categorised from Universal to R18, meaning the ViM can be shown only in specially licensed Memory Bank facilities and only to adults over 18 years of age. I'm able to identify a title for the kind of adventure the Knick-Knack tramp would have been involved in pretty easily. In fact, I'm even surprised Fiskdale included it in the menu, just as I'm surprised he offered a menu in the first place. Perhaps it's because it's a 15 and the idea was that Jonas would only select a PG. Whatever, the fact is the ViM had nothing to do with volcanoes or semi-beings and everything to do with, well with Christmas. It was categorised a Self Esteem Memory and uploaded by Tom Crabb, who's in P3 at school. The title? Santa *Tramp*, otherwise I'd have missed it. I'll read out the transcript to you.

Tom Crabb had been queuing patiently for over an hour to see Santa at the North Pole, sponsored by Good Green Energy, the Company Helping the Arctic Keep Cool. He'd never met Santa before and hoped he wouldn't be scared because he usually finds men with beards scary. At long last it's his turn and he steps up onto the platform and gives Santa his best smile. Since actual physical contact between Santa and the children queuing was banned five years ago, smiling is the only way for juniors to express their feelings. Tom gave Santa his very best smile he'd been practising in the bathroom mirror all week and said he was very pleased to meet him. Santa asked Tom what he'd like for Christmas and Tom said lots of snout fillers, snack stoppers and third ways please thank you very much Santa.

Santa told Tom Crabb this was just as well because he'd been shopping in a special area of Lapland called Delice-Stanley-Bahm and his helper handed him a sack of goodies for Tom to take away. Tom was really delighted and thanked Santa with his best smile. He was so happy he moved closer to Santa to give him a bow and it was then that he saw what looked like spirits in the bottle of Slam juice at Santa's feet and smelled alcohol on his breath. He only knew this because Uncle Jasper smelled the same way at Christmas after he'd drunk too much sherry and started talking too loudly when everybody could hear him perfectly well already.

When he was out of the Good Green Energy Grotto he told his dad what he'd seen, who told a representative from Delice-Stanley-Bahm, who had a sniff of the Slam bottle while Santa was handing Grace Delilly tickets to see The Chocolate Nutcracker at the Royal Emirates Ballet.

Events moved swiftly after this. A screen was placed around Santa's Good Green Energy Grotto, though Tom was able to peer through the join between the boards. He was shocked to see that Santa was not actually Santa but an elderly man who dressed like a tramp under his Santa outfit and protested his innocence before admitting that a little nip helped keep him in character. After the fake Santa was ejected from the building the Delice-Stanley-Bahm representative opened up the Good Green Energy Grotto and announced that a young hero called Tom Crabb had uncovered Santa as a fraud and will be receiving a year's supply of snout fillers without any impact on his family's Health Account. Tom came up to the podium to receive a snout filler as a token of his prize, which he raised above his head in victory and to thunderous applause.

Well, you don't need me to tell you the identity of Tom Crabb's fake Santa. In fact, this ViM was probably how Fiskdale met Adrian Gulp in the first place. He'd be on the lookout for somebody to play all the different roles in the Secret Room, somebody desperate for easy money he could wrap around his little finger. Giles would keep an eye out for any likely candidates at the Memory Bank and probably gave him this ViM, thinking it was useful in any case because it showed Delice-Stanley-Bahm in a bad light.

The tricky thing now was to identify a connection between Jonas' Scary Man ViM and Tom Crabb's Santa Tramp ViM. I racked my brain. Perhaps there wasn't one and they just happened to be ViMs Fiskdale had in his collection because he liked them. But no, that couldn't be it. There was something more, otherwise why would he go to such lengths to get a hold of Jonas' Scary Man ViM.

Then I realised because I didn't have to upload a memory to access Tom Crabb's ViM I had time for one more download. It was a lot to take on board at once because actually experiencing ViMs is ten times more tiring than uploading them but this opportunity wasn't going to come around again. I scanned the list of titles to see one that might bring more light to whatever it was Mr Fiskdale was up to. Most of the ViMs had really weird names like Lady Of The Lake, Peat Bog Man and Guido's Night but I selected one that at least sounded like it had a connection with meteorology, an Adventure ViM called Rainstorm Girl. I'm going to have to tell you about Rainstorm Girl myself instead of reading out the transcript because there isn't one available.

Mrs Audrey Campbell, sub-Postmistress of Danemore Post Office, is driving home after spending the evening with her sister Deirdre, who lives in the village of Frittingham, three miles south of Danemore. It's a dark and stormy night of torrential rain and thunder and lightening so she drives slowly but there's nothing she can do about the girl running across the road in front of her. The girl stares into the headlights and her pale face, red hair and green eyes burn into Audrey's mind.

Audrey swerves to avoid her, but must have swerved the wrong way in panic because she hits the girl. She stops and sits in the car for several minutes, trembling so much it takes her three attempts to open the door. She fetches a torch from the boot and sees the girl's body in the road fifty metres behind her. She's wearing a white dress with a blood red stain spreading across it. Moving closer she notices the girl's chest rising and realises she's alive. She kneels down and the girl mutters something, but she can only make out the word 'call'. It sounds as though the girl is trying to give Audrey an instruction to call somebody. Then she dies.

Audrey drives to Danemore Police Station and the officer on night duty returns with her to the scene of the accident. The body is no longer there and not a trace of blood remains. Audrey is confused and looks over her car but the dent in the bonnet is also gone.

In the morning she returns to the Station to write out an incident report. When she finishes Superintendent Holmes asks her to step into his office, where Dr Bradley from the Psychiatric Unit of Danemore Hospital joins them. Dr Bradley informs Audrey that on the 16th of June 1983 Hannah Dyson suffered a fatal crash in heavy rain on the stretch of road where the accident happened. She was on her way to be married at Danemore United Church. Ever since, around that time of year in heavy rain, there have been sightings of a young girl in white running across the road. In other words, Audrey had just seen Hannah Dyson's ghost.

13 Wedding Dress

What did you make of that last ViM then? Okay, so it might not be scary to hear about, but it was truly terrifying to experience. You're right there in the car when suddenly this figure comes out of nowhere. You're focusing on the road ahead because of how dark it is and all that rain and the last thing you expect is for a girl in a wedding dress to jump out at you. Made all the weirder by the dress being one of those puffy Eighties ones like you see in retro TV shows, sort of a blancmange on legs. And the girl's face is so close, with her tiara and red hair all wet with rain and big green eyes and make up running. Then the bump as she hits you, like when Dad runs over an animal in the road but lots worse. Shot through with horror film special effects, rolls of thunder and claps of lightening. Plus, I don't know the first thing about how to drive a car. I mean, the ViM should at least be an 18 since you can't even get a provisional license until you're 17.

To give Fiskdale his due, I can see why he was so concerned about Jonas experiencing ViMs like this. I've not actually seen it, but I'm guessing his Scary Man ViM is Mickey Mouse compared to Rainstorm Girl. In fact, the ViM hit me so hard I had to lie down for a bit and listen to some nice calming music to recover when we got home. Later that evening I checked out the story at Danemore Public Library online archives and read three separate accounts of Rainstorm Girl, all taking place on the same stretch of

119

road at the same time of year and in similar weather conditions. I also read the original report of Hannah Dyson's death. The car taking her to the church hit a tree by the side of the road when visibility was down to ten metres and the driver was going too fast to make up the time. Neither survived.

One of the newspaper reports included a sketch of how the girl looked according to the first person to see her run across the road. This was then used for later witnesses to corroborate their own experiences. To corroborate something means to support what you're saying using other evidence. Both witnesses said the girl in the sketch was the spitting image of the one they saw. I printed out the sketch and stuck it on the board by the computer in my room. It happened to be a very good likeness of the girl in the Rainstorm Girl ViM and I thought it'd make a handy reference for when I returned to the Secret Room. I never imagined it would have a more direct use until Mum came in for my washing.

I was working away on my computer at the time. Mum usually leaves right after collecting the clothes from my basket but this time I could feel her hovering.

'Where did you get that on the board there?' she asked.

'Where did I get what, Mum?'

It was obvious what she was meaning because everything else had been up there for weeks, but I really didn't want to make a big thing of the sketch.

'The printout.'

'Oh, that's my dance schedule for the summer holidays.'

'Not that, silly. The sketch of the girl in the wedding dress. Where did you get it?'

'Found it on the Internet. Remember we're doing an Eighties show at the end of term. I just thought it was a classic Eighties dress I could maybe make use of somehow.'

'Why didn't you come to me then? Isn't your mother the resident Eighties expert of all things tacky and tasteless?'

'I suppose.'

'For instance, that dress there. I had to make a dress just like it for a client only a few months ago.'

'You what!'

I swivelled round in my chair.

'Just as I said. You know how I do these one off jobs for clients every now and then? Well this was one of them. Which reminds me, I've still not got paid for it.'

'Hold on, Mum. This is important. I can't tell you why, but it's really important. Can you go back and tell me all about it from the start.'

I couldn't believe what I heard. Turns out Mum had a meeting with Fiskdale about the dress two months ago. So he knew all about Mum and had actually visited the house long before we met. He took a real risk coming to the door after we hadn't sent him Jonas' Scary Man ViM that time. And to think I'd been so relieved Mum hadn't seen him. What a cool customer he was. If she'd seen him I was sure I'd be a lot further along with my investigations than I was now. The good news was Mum still had the name and address of where she sent the finished dress, which just so happened to be of an actress called Janet Low who looked identical to the Rainstorm Girl. Things were beginning to connect up. The problem now was Janet Low lived in London and I lived in Danemore. Plus I was grounded.

'So where did you send the bill, Mum?'

'Why, to Mr Fiskdale of course.'

'Aha, then that's why you've not been paid. We've been studying Economics at school and there's a new rule now that payment can only be sent to the same address where you deliver the goods.'

'What rot, Milly. Pull the other one.'

I had to admit this was one of my weaker efforts, especially since we don't do Economics at School and Mum knew it. Not only that, but I'd now managed to flag my unusual interest in Janet Low and Mum's dress. It was time to fess up.

'Okay, Mum, the thing is I saw a ViM that had something to do with this dress. Have you ever heard of Hannah Dyson?'

Don't worry, I didn't tell her lots. But I did tell her about the Rainstorm Girl and how much it scared me. To overcome my fear I did some research and read about the tragedy of Hannah Dyson. I also told her I looked up Miss Low after what she told me about the dress and was struck by her resemblance to Hannah Dyson and worried about getting nightmares like the one I had last night (we're now into Sunday) unless I actually met Miss Low to confirm one hundred percent she'd nothing to do with Hannah Dyson.

'Goodness, Milly,' Mum said, 'I don't know what's got into this family these days. No sooner has Jonas settled down than you are off on some nonsense about a poor woman who died years ago. I think it's time your dad and I looked again at these trips to the Memory Bank. In the meantime, you're still grounded.'

It was a long shot, but at least it got Mum's attention and she agreed to contact Miss Low next time we were in London. Obviously this wasn't soon enough so I had a series of really noisy screaming nightmares on Sunday, Monday and Tuesday nights. That did it. We drove down to London after school on Wednesday and arranged to meet Miss Low in the café of the theatre where she worked in the West End.

*

'I'm afraid I can only give you ten minutes, darlings,' Miss Low said, stirring milk into the tea Mum poured out for her. 'I'm due in make up in fifteen.'

'That's quite alright,' said Mum. 'Thank you so much for making the time to see us. I'm sure you have a busy schedule.'

'Things are rather quiet during the day actually, unless we have a matinee of course, which we do on Thursdays and Saturdays. The rest of the time I walk Cedric to keep active. You see my character is a poor girl with a broken heart who lies in bed all day and only gets up in the last act to eat a cupcake. I wouldn't mind so much if it were something healthy like a rice cake, but a *cupcake*, darlings. I asked for a change and the director called the writer who threw a hissy fit saying it had to be a cupcake because it symbolised a brighter, more colourful future for the character and a rice cake was neither colourful nor bright. I mean, *please*.'

We both stared blankly.

'Cedric is my poodle of course, not some fellow I've picked up off the street. Oh no. Although picking someone up off the street is perhaps the only solution now I'm officially nearing the big three oh.'

I tried to follow all this but had not the foggiest idea what she was talking about, although it sounded wonderful coming from her bright red glossy lips.

'And read any of the scripts my agent sends me. Curiously, I often find my life is as interesting as the character I'm playing and this one, well you can imagine. So how can I help? What is it you want to know?'

There was a long pause until I realised both Miss Low and Mum were looking at me. To be honest I was miles away, checking out the posters on the walls of all the famous performances taking place here over the years, trying to imagine the relationship between the smartly dressed black man and beautiful woman in the corner, gazing at all those lovely pastries on the cake stand by the counter, admiring the little Japanese clips inlaid with lacquer in Miss Low's hair, enjoying the classical music playing softly in the background. I was in paradise and thinking how much I wanted to enter this world of style and glamour and beautiful things. It made me want to practice harder than ever for my ballet exams at the end of August. They were still a long way off but there was plenty of work to be done in preparation.

'What? Sorry?' I sat up and returned to the here and now. 'Okay. Right. Well, the thing is I don't understand what you have to do with Hannah Dyson. I mean you look just like her and my mum made you the wedding dress she wore when she died. To be honest, it's been giving me really bad nightmares where I think you're her ghost returned from the dead and you come into my room and attack me with a tiara. You'll understand about the tiara if you've seen Rainstorm Girl.'

Mum was looking deadly serious but I swear I saw a flicker of a snigger cross Miss Low's beautiful face.

'I see,' Miss Low said, stirring her tea as she considered her reply. 'The first thing you should know is I've actually seen Rainstorm Girl. Mr Fiskdale, who hired me for the job, showed it to me as preparation for the part. I have to admit my resemblance to Hannah Dyson did give me the jitters, especially considering the way she died. Lucky girl, I say, but also poor thing. A tragic ending, I think you'll agree, darlings. So I was a little shall we say *unnerved* to play the part, but it was only an afternoon's work because that's all they could afford of me. Actually it was lower than my usual rate since it was for a good cause.'

'A good cause?' Mum said. 'How so?'

'You see the concept of the piece was road safety. I've not seen the finished film, but at least that was what I was led to believe it was about.'

'So what did Mr Fish Head get you to do? Sorry for being so nosy, but I think it'll really help me with my nightmares. All these horrid pictures have built up in my mind and the best way to get them out again is to have a new set of pictures.'

'Right,' said Miss Low, sounding unconvinced. 'First of all, it's not Mr Fish Head, darling. It's Mr Fiskdale. Quite simple really. We went to this stretch of road with a bend in it like the one in Rainstorm Girl, even though you couldn't really see it because of all that rain. It was quite a bother to set up because we had to wait for a rainy day and work very quickly from that. I do so much prefer working indoors when weather isn't a factor.

I was in the back seat with this sweet little girl called Darcy and the camera was in the passenger seat. Darcy was such a sweetheart, and much easier to work with than most of my leading men. I don't know where that old adage about children and animals comes from because I'm sure I could work with Cedric just as well.

It was all shot backwards to be edited forwards for some reason. First of all they got lots of shots of Darcy and me in the backseat, Darcy in her child seat and me with my seatbelt on. I complained it looked like I was on my way down the altar with a child in tow, but I don't suppose this matters so much these days. Darcy was very good because we sat there for hours waiting for the right sort of light and she never complained once. In fact, we spent most of the time playing I Spy, although there wasn't much to spy of course. Luckily I've always had an immediate connection with children so we were able to fill out the time quite easily.

Then at the end of the day we shot an exterior of me carrying Darcy to the car and strapping her in the child seat. You see the idea was to promote a particular brand of child seats, a sort of 'if Hannah Dyson did one thing different' scenario. Seemed a peculiar concept to me but Mr Fiskdale said it would work just fine and this was the way adverts were going in the age of ViMs. And that's it, darlings, but now I simply have to run or I'll be late. After all, the show must go on.'

'Did you get paid?' Mum asked.

'Absolutely. It's written in my contract always to be paid up front.'

I asked what the make of child seat was and Miss Low said she thought it was something beginning with E. Then she stood and collected her things from the table. Standing to her full height, she was much taller than I imagined, just like Fiskdale was.

'Don't you know you can't trust anyone in this day and age, darlings?'

And then she was off, leaving a sweet smell of perfume behind.

I dozed on the way home and only woke when Mum pulled into a garage off the motorway to charge the car. She brought me a packet of my favourite snout fillers from the shop.

'Feeling better now?' she asked. 'No more bad dreams?'

'No more bad dreams,' I said. 'Thanks to you, Mummy. By the way, do you still have the measurements for that dress?'

14 Housework

It's Thursday night and I'm beat. So much has happened this week just keeping up is a full time job. Add to this my forfeit and homework and ballet and Eighties night and the final few weeks of Primary School ever. So it's crazy I'm spending all my free time recording this, especially when I don't even know why I'm doing it. Is it to get the facts down in case anything happens to Jonas or me? Is it because I can smell a rat and he just won't go away? Or is it simply out of habit, like Jonas and his computer games, but better for you. After all, it's an amazing story, like I said. But it might be more fun to hear about than tell.

Anyway, it's the reason I'm tired tonight. We only got back around nine thirty last night after stopping for fish and tofu on the way home. I had maths to do but first I recorded our meeting with Miss Low when it was still fresh in my mind. Only the computer crashed before I saved it so I had to start all over again and it wasn't done until after eleven. Then I had two pages of fractions to do, which were tricky and boring. I tell you, if being an adult's anything like this I think I'll pass. At least I slept well because I didn't have to stay up half the night pretending to have nightmares.

The morning brought some exciting news, though. Budi Noors is coming to stay with us for a few days later in the month. In fact, he'll be here the same week as Eighties night. Mum took an early call from the British Embassy in Jakarta. Because the Noors showed the biggest increase in the production of sustainable organic goods of any sponsored business blah, blah, blah, one family member gets an all expenses paid trip to the UK. Mr Noors chose Budi as a special treat for coming first in his English test at school. Apparently he's almost fluent, which is kind of amazing considering he's a year younger than me. He's arriving on Tuesday the sixteenth and staying four days before moving to a London hotel for three nights and then flying home. I think this is excellent news. First of all it will be great to see Budi and secondly it might be fun to dress him up for Eighties night.

All afternoon at school was spent preparing for this night, which is just around the corner. It's important I make a decent stab of it because we perform in front of the whole school and it's our swansong before leaving. A swansong is the end of something forever, though don't ask me what swans and songs have to do with this. The idea came from some bright spark who found out that the average age of a P7 parent was forty one, making 1985 their birth year. As a result the headteacher, Mr Randolph, decided our final year show should be a celebration of the Eighties, even though we were born yonks later. It's a pretty lame idea and I think Mr Randolph chose it because he was young in the Eighties, so it's like a trip down memory lane for him but irrelevant for everybody else.

It was a slow afternoon, working in a group that included Sarah Fiddle and Casper and Cassie Cruise, the terrible twins. Casper and Cassie are known as the terrible twins because if you start an argument with one of them you'll end it with both. They back each other up, finish each other's sentences and always have twice as many points as you, even when they're obviously wrong and the argument is really silly. Today they were at their most annoying.

Our homework was to design an outfit for Eighties night based on a well-known Eighties celebrity. You then had to act out a scene in character, besides original footage from the Eighties. Sarah Fiddle was Madonna, the Cruises were the boy band Bros and I was Princess Diana. Sarah Fiddle looked nothing like Madonna and failed to sing, act or dance convincingly during her performance of Like A Prayer. The Cruise's fundamental problem was that Bros were two blonde brothers when they both had dark hair and Cassie was a girl. Thank goodness it was Casper who sang Drop The Boy because it's about becoming a man, something that is never going to happen to Cassie unless something really weird happens.

'Yeah, we're calling ourselves Sibs actually,' Cassie said. 'You know, like a more modern, non-sexist version of Bros.'

'We've got the denim and earrings,' added Casper.

'And Casper is really good at hitting the high notes, better than the original singer as a matter of fact.'

'And Cassie is really good at drumming.'

'We've got the hats and leather jackets.'

'What about the hair then?'

'Not an issue because Sibs is not Bros, is it?'

'And we can get hair dye.'

'Or wear wigs.'

'But it's not an issue anyway because we're Sibs not Bros.'

What with the events of last night and everything else going on I wasn't really prepared for Eighties night and only had two ideas for a scene. One was the Royal Wedding, which was boring, and the other was dancing with John Travolta at the White House, where the American President lives. Dancing with the guy from Grease and Saturday Night Fever, Mum's two favourite movies, sounds pretty cool, but Princess Diana wore a black dress then and I spent the whole morning before school explaining how I'd only be able to do Eighties night if Mum made me Hannah Dyson's dress to wear for the Royal Wedding.

It's stuff like this that's really starting to annoy me. In other words, because I'm doing my public duty investigating someone's dodgyness I have to turn down the man Mum had pictures of on her bedroom wall as a child for our ancient King, or the Prince of Wales as he was then. Bit like kissing a frog that turns into a prince, but the other way round. At least it's a good reason for getting the dress made. Everything was working like clockwork in that respect. It was just a pity that my next job was to find somebody to play Prince Charles rather than John Travolta.

Back home I had three loads of laundry to put through the washing machine and hang out to dry. You get used to this after a while and wonder where all the time went before. I mean it's not like I'm Jonas, wired up to a games console every minute of the day. Now it's gone nine and I've filled you in on everything that's happened and I'm having an early night, head filled with connections and plans. Connections between semi-beings, Santa Tramps and Rainstorm Girls, between Knick-Knacks and child seats, between Amy and Fish Head and Jonas. Plans for what to do on my return to Holbalm Hall in the morning and how to use Budi Noors. Connections and plans, plans and connections, connections and plans. Goodnight and thank you for listening.

*

Amazing. Simply amazing. Things have just stepped up a gear. I managed to get out of our annual Nature Walk and have a good rummage round Holbalm Hall today. It was so easy. The whole school was going on this walk so I didn't think I'd be missed so long as I was there at the beginning and the end. The tricky bit was at lunchtime when the roll call is taken. For this I gave Fiona Fudge a bag of snack stoppers to call out my name and be near Mrs Lolly with a ready answer whenever she wondered where I was. Alf waited for me in our usual spot round from the school gates and I was over the wall and into the grounds of Holbalm Hall by first break. I thought it best to retrace my steps from last time. I went round the hedge and was making my way through the Hall towards the Secret Room when I walked straight into a mantelpiece.

Fiskdale had the builders in, or however you describe it when you replace a virtual room with an original. I was dazed and sat down on a chair to recover. I wasn't thinking about the risk involved, but the chair held firm and I didn't fly through the air and land on my bum. Soon I was knocking on tables, running fingers over paintings and switching lights on and off. I sniffed the flowers arranged in a vase on the mantelpiece and tinkled a few notes on the Baby Grand looking out towards the maze. No doubt about it. I was in a real room. I opened the door and found another room, then another and another.

Where did the money come for this? Fiskdale's basic problem was that apart from his confectionary stash he was broke. He most likely paid Adrian Gulp in booze just as Gulp said he did. He ordered taxis, but that was probably paid in kind too. He was after all a weather presenter who no longer presented the weather. I was only in Holbalm Hall a week ago and it was entirely virtual, right down to the nasty toilet cubicles in the Servants Wing that Jonas raced me through. Where did the money come for this? What had changed since? The only thing I could think of was that Fiskdale got hold of Jonas' ViM. Could this have made the difference? Was Jonas' ViM the last piece in the jigsaw of Fiskdale's dastardly plans?

These are the questions I wished I asked myself at the time, but I got distracted. C'mon, I was in a mansion on my own and a cool one where some rooms were real and some were not. I'd just had the best sleep in ages and was fighting fit from doing my forfeit chores. Nobody did any work on the Nature Walk, so why should I at Holbalm Hall? It was playtime.

By lunchtime I'd done a full recce and found sixteen real rooms. All those hours trailing through stately homes with Mum and Dad paid off because I was able to identify the types of rooms they were. The room with the piano and mantelpiece I banged into was the Drawing Room, a bit like a posh Sitting Room but much bigger. A corridor led to the Dining Room. This was one of the easier ones to identify because of the sideboard and tables and chairs. There was even a candlestick and bowl of fresh fruit on the table and napkins laid out.

Where there's a Dining Room there's usually a kitchen, but everybody knows kitchens are expensive. Maybe the budget couldn't stretch to this and all cooking was done back at

Fiskdale's gatehouse. Anyway, I couldn't find it, despite knowing it wouldn't be anywhere near the Dining Room because we studied the Victorians at school and learned big houses had lots of staff who did loads of pointless fetching and carrying to earn their keep.

Found three bedrooms though, and a Billiard Room that had been turned into a dormitory. The bedrooms were nice, nicer than any I'd seen before apart from the ones in stately homes even larger than Holbalm Hall. They were modernised too, with en suite bathrooms including lovely big baths and baskets of towels and soap and lotion sachets. So how many are we up to now? Drawing Room, Dining Room, Billiard Room, three en suite bedrooms. Nine. I'm sure there's more than that.

The Nursery. I almost forgot the Nursery. Actually the Nursery was three rooms, one with old-fashioned toys and one with modern toys and one made into a soft play area. I reckoned most of the money was spent here. Some thought had been put into how to organise the space so kids could have fun and feel safe at the same time. All the kit was top of the range and brand new. I spent loads of time playing with stuff that must have just come on the market because I'd never seen it before. This might be because I was at the age it was designed for ten years ago though. It was all pre-school stuff for toddlers and babies, and I'm sure if I were a toddler or a baby I'd have loved it.

Eventually I had to drag myself away because time was running short and a great idea came into my head. Let Fiskdale see somebody's been here and knows what he's up to. I went back to the Drawing Room and started moving things about. Then I returned to the Dining Room and put all the chairs upside down on the dining table. I grew bolder as I went on. I went to the bedrooms and swapped labels on the soap and shampoo dispensers and used the bathroom scissors to cut strands of my hair to scatter on the pillow.

I still had twenty minutes before Alf was due to pick me up. One thing I noticed was there were an awful lot of pictures about. In the Drawing Room there were horrible pictures of naked people in all sorts of weird poses that looked like they'd been painted ages ago. I unhooked as many as I could carry and went to the Nursery, where the walls were covered with cartoon animals, scenes from Walt Disney Pictures and adverts for Homemaker Industries products. I just had time to swap them around before running to be on time for Alf. A quarter to three I was picking up my school bag and wishing Mrs Lolly a good weekend.

After dinner I had a quick look at Google Live Cam to see whether Holbalm Hall looked any different now. Just as I expected, it didn't. Then I moved over to the site of the Secret Room, feeling guilty I never made it there when it was the main reason I went back. There it was, the same old patch of bare grass just behind Fiskdale's gatehouse. Something was different though. The land the Secret Room sat on was always clearly defined because it was surrounded by grass left to grow wild. I always remembered this because I didn't think it was very clever of Fiskdale to leave things like this considering the number of nosy parkers using Google Live Cam. But now there's a second patch of bare grass twice the size of the Secret Room patch. There couldn't be a second Secret Room at Holbalm Hall, could there?

15 SLOB

I think the best way to do this is as a writing exercise. You know, the kind at school where you have WALT and WILF. If you've not met them, WALT and WILF are two characters that stand for We Are Learning To and What I'm Looking For. They remind you what it is your teacher wants you to do. Some people think they're silly and only for little kids, but I find them helpful. So we are learning to describe SLOB in as much detail as possible in order to help the police with their investigations. And to be used as corroborative evidence for when Fiskdale gets arrested, which hopefully isn't too far away. What I'm looking for are clues and signs telling me what's going on. This isn't really what WILF means, but you'll get the idea soon enough.

Another trick is to think about the why, who, where, what, when and how of what it is you're writing. Where you know already and I don't think I have to tell you why by now. Who is Jonas and me, when is Saturday morning and how is by bribing Jonas with sweeties and telling Mum there's a rehearsal for Eighties night at a friend's house and I need Jonas to come along to be my King Charles, or Prince Charles as he was. I wish I'd taken a notebook for the what, but I've got a pretty good idea of what I saw anyway. Luckily nobody collapsed this time so we were able to walk around the building and look through all the windows. There were quite a few so we could see what was going on from different angles, getting a sort of 360 view of the room.

137

Before we start let me explain that I've renamed the second Secret Room. This is because calling it the second Secret Room is silly. It's too close to the Secret Room, which is confusing, and it doesn't actually describe what happens in it. From now on I'm going to call it the Secret Laboratory of Babies, or SLOB for short. It's a lab for toddlers too, but SLOBT just doesn't have the same ring somehow.

From what me and Jonas can tell SLOB runs experiments on babies and toddlers to check how they respond to the films made in the Secret Room immediately after experiencing one of Fiskdale's ViMs. Duh, this is so obvious I don't know why I didn't think about it before. I was so hung up on what the ViMs were about I never considered how they made you *feel*. Basically, the connection between the Scary Man and Rainstorm Girl ViMs is that they both scare you witless. So when you see the same characters in films with sweeties and car seats, you're put off the sweeties and car seats for life. A bit like advertising, but the opposite. Anti-advertising, if you like, illegal and highly dangerous for little ones. Which makes Fiskdale some sort of evil genius. I'm getting away from WALT and WILF though.

SLOB is built on the back of Fiskdale's gatehouse just like the Secret Room was, though we couldn't see a door connecting the two. In fact, we couldn't find the Secret Room at all and think it must have been packed up and shipped off, or whatever it is that happens to invisible rooms after they're no longer useful. Fiskdale wouldn't want to leave evidence behind and invisible rooms are probably as easy to spirit away as they are to set up. I reckon the same thing will happen to SLOB, which is why I'm describing it in detail now.

There's an entire wall of Memory Bank capsules to the left as you enter SLOB from the gatehouse, three rows of four going up to the ceiling. Just operating one capsule uses more energy than an average family gets through in a week, so you can imagine how much energy it takes to operate twelve. Especially when they're as busy as they were today, fed by a constant stream of pushchairs, buggies and prams driven by Mums and Dads eager to load their little ones into capsules. The reason for this becomes clear when you look over to the exit, where families are given large boxes of Homemaker Industries products on their way out. Both lines are heavily staffed, with passports checked and bags, prams and bodies searched.

Mum and Dad sign a form and everybody gets their picture taken before the parents are told which capsule to put their little darling into. Jonas timed how long they were in the capsule and it came out at twenty minutes, enough for one upload or two downloads. Usually you get half an hour to manage both, but my guess is Fiskdale isn't interested in uploads and provides just enough time for two downloads. I learned the other day how knackering this is and I'm twelve, so you can imagine the affect it has on a two year old. Which must be what Fiskdale wants.

After they finish, the little ones go to an area that looks like a mini mall with a small café and tiny cinema. Many look lost and anxious and a few are crying as they're taken out of their capsules. Not that the parents really notice. The family is then split up again, Mums and Dads to the café and children to the cinema. I'm guessing the café is free judging by the amount of Homemaker Industries products parents stuff into their gobs, cram into bags and stash under jumpers. Gallons of coffee are also drunk. Meanwhile, the babies and toddlers sit in the cinema and watch something probably totally wrong for their age group, though the programme by the curtained entrance advertises Wallis In Wonderland, a film about a cartoon whale called Wallis who discovers an extra terrestrial shipwreck at the bottom of the sea. I know this because I've seen Wallis In Wonderland. It isn't very good.

Jonas reckoned the cinema session also lasted twenty minutes, when a cinema usher collects the child and takes them to a desk in the middle of the room. A lady there asks the child's name and looks it up on a chart before telling them to go to a particular booth.

The booths are set up to present familiar products in the settings you'd normally find them. For instance the booth containing child seats looks just like the kind of shop you'd visit to buy a child seat, with prices and displays and everything. There are tills and prams on stands with Homemaker Industries adverts everywhere and even a few rails featuring items for sale like kiddie clothes and nappies.

Some booths are really cool, especially the sweetie ones. These booths range from a version of the cafe where the Mums and Dads are gorging themselves to gyms with vending machines and newsagents like the ones on the High Street. Basically all the different types of places licensed to sell products with high sugar content. The one I like best features the inside of an airplane with an air stewardess pushing her trolley down the aisle selling duty free sweets. The TV in the aisle shows ads for Homemaker Industries products, there are sick bags behind each seat and even buttons overhead telling you when to strap up and turn off lights.

As you'll have worked out by now, we got a really good view of these booths. Each booth has a window looking into it from the corridor so we saw everything as clearly as the two assessors sitting directly below us on the other side of the wall. The booths also had enough CCTV cameras to catch each moment from a dozen different angles. The shop assistants are clearly aware of this because they never get between the children and the observers and mostly stay crouched down out of the way.

Jonas and me watched three different scenarios. By and large we were able to agree about what we thought happened in the two we watched together. In each the usher brought the little one into the booth and introduced them to the shop assistant. The parents were already there or arrived shortly after. Everybody acted like they were in a real shop so the little girl or boy would act naturally and look around to see what they could get their hands on.

In the booth designed to look like a shop selling child seats, the shop assistant approached the family. I admit we couldn't hear what was said, but I'm guessing she asked if they needed any help or were just browsing. Mum probably said they were looking for a child seat and asked what was available. The shop assistant then showed them two child seats, an Eazy Seat and a Rhapsody made by Stiehls. The little girl started screaming as soon as she saw the Eazy Seat and pleaded with her parents to get the Rhapsody seat. Could Eazy Seat be the brand name beginning with E Miss Low said featured in the film she made with Fiskdale, and Stiehls a Homemaker Industries company? These were things to check out.

The second booth Jonas and me saw looked like the entrance to a leisure centre, and was so real I even thought I smelled that funny stuff they put in swimming pools to make them more hygienic. There was a gate with a counter where you had to pay and opposite was a bank of vending machines. Obviously this wasn't staffed and all Dad had to do was pick Junior up to show him what was for sale and get him to make a selection. Because the machine was real but the situation wasn't he didn't have to put his card in to pay and have the items count against his Health Account. This put Dad in such a good mood he overlooked the violent reaction Junior had to certain products. Once again the kid picked Homemaker Industries products, including a packet of Y-nots over the thousand times more popular Knick-Knacks, something that would never happen in reality. Of course, I knew what this was all about after seeing the Santa Tramp ViM and Adrian Gulp making the advert for Knick-Knacks in the Secret Room.

I saw a similar thing in the supermarket booth, where the child was held up to choose a cone or ice-lolly from the fridge. While I watched the little girl throw a wobbly and start squirming in her mum's arms after seeing a particular brand of ice-lolly, Jonas was over at the toyshop booth. The parents and shop assistant let the child run riot there until she came across the Stuffed Dolls section. She searched out a doll from the Princess range dressed in a pink tutu and matching leotard, but only after making sure the entire range of Jolly Dolls were out of sight right at the back of the shelves. Jolly Dolls and Princess Dolls, two more items to check out.

In every scenario the child was given time to make a selection, with the parent or shop assistant asking questions about it. Unfortunately we couldn't hear what was said but got an idea through body language, which obviously there needs to be lots of to communicate with little ones just learning to speak. Before and after the little ones made their choice similar products were held up, often to crying and tantrums and other extreme reactions. One child threw the packet of crisps she was given on the floor and started throwing cans and stamping on it, another held tightly on to Mummy before the product was removed from sight.

We realised this was the final stage when we followed one family from a booth all the way to the exit and their box of Homemaker Industries products. By now it was getting close to lunch and the time Mum and Dad expected us home. We'd seen enough for one day anyway, which was quite an incredible day, when you think about it. The day it finally became clear exactly what Fiskdale was up to. I just wish we could be made invisible like one of these secret rooms. Then we'd wander around and check details, listen to conversations and sit in the tiny cinema to see exactly what's playing. I'd be very surprised if it wasn't the films Fiskdale shot in the Secret Room with the same characters from the scary ViMs, but it'd be good to make sure.

I figure the next step is to find one of the toddlers who'd gone through the whole SLOB experience and ask them about the ViM they experienced and what they saw in the tiny cinema. So it's just as well I recognised one of the Mums and Dads stuffing themselves in the small café. Mr and Mrs Drabble are the parents of Max, who is in my year at school. More importantly they are the parents of Sandra, who I remember being born during our end of term camp two years ago. Summer camp always happens around mid-June, so Sandra must be coming up for two, the ideal SLOB age. Even though he was really, really annoying, it was time to make friends with Max Drabble.

16 Parrots

Max Drabble isn't hard to get close to. This is because Max Drabble has wanted to get close to me ever since P5. I know because he told me so. After I'd spotted a horrid fantasy book in his locker and asked him to borrow it when he was done. After he said he'd finished it and would give it to me during computer club. After boring me to tears for an hour about his gaming adventures at computer club. After asking how Sandra's doing and being invited round to see her. After saying I'd love to. Great, he says, I've wanted to ask you round ever since P5. I don't know. The sacrifices I make. First I've got to turn down John Travolta for Prince Charles, now I've got to hang out with Max Drabble, geekiest geek of all the geeks in geekdom.

The next thing is persuading Mum to let me go round on a school night. To do this I actually tell her the truth, or something like it. A good friend has a new baby sister and I want to meet her.

'Who's the friend?' asks Mum.

'Max Drabble.'

'I've not heard that name before.'

'I see him loads at school. For example, I was at computer club with him just today. We get on great. Anyway, his mum's had a baby girl and I want to go round and see her. You know how I am with babies.'

'Oh, I know how you are with babies, as long as they're not that poor little cousin of yours. Really, you must be try to be nicer to Ellen next time.'

'I will. C'mon, Mum.'

'Promise me, because I don't want another Christmas like the last one.'

When Jonas and me taped wrapping paper all over Baby Ellen and attached a card saying Return to Sender.

'Promise.'

Mum was in the middle of stitching the hem of my Eighties wedding dress. The best thing now was to give her time to think. So I just stood there and waited.

'Well, you have been working really hard at your forfeit. And it is almost the end of term. Even though you're naughty for going to the computer club when we told you no after school clubs. I'll let you go this once. You're in luck because Dad's so happy his team got through to the semis of the World Cup I'm sure he'll be glad to drive you there and back.'

'Excellent, Mum. Thank you *so* much.'

'And maybe next time Max will come round here and we'll all get a chance to meet him.'

*

The Drabbles don't live too far away, on a new estate near Danemore Leisure Centre. They live in an average house on an average street in an average area. There's nothing average about their house inside though. This is because the Drabbles keep Parrots, but not the way average people keep Parrots. In fact, average people no longer keep Parrots since it was made illegal to use cages. This put average people off, but not the Drabbles.

'That's funny, I didn't think it snowed in June,' Dad said as we approached the gate and saw the front garden covered in white.

His smile fell when we reached the door and he realised it wasn't snow but bird droppings. Later I discovered a top window was left open for the Parrots to go and do their business outside. Dad was just about to ring the doorbell when he noticed a sign on the door.

Hello. Howdy. Bonjour. Konnichiwa. Pleased to meet you, or if we've met before nice to see you again. Kindly walk in AS quietly AP because excessive noise like bell ringing or knuckle knocking upsets Queen Victoria and the Prince Consort.

Mrs Drabble must have heard us come in because she rushed down the stairs to say hello. She wore an apron she dried herself on before shaking hands. Her hair and shoulders were covered in red, blue and yellow feathers and she looked flustered.

'Please excuse me,' she said. 'I've just been bathing the Prince Consort. He gets this daily in the jungles of Costa Rica, you see, so I try to keep it up in grey old Danemore. The water has to be exactly 25 degrees otherwise he gets in a flap.'

'Right,' said Dad, one of the few times I'd seen him lost for words.

'You must be Milly,' said Mrs Drabble. 'So nice to finally meet you. Max has told us so much about you.'

'Right,' said Dad. 'Best be off then. I'll call to see when you want picked up.'

'No calls here, Mr Buntly,' said Mrs Drabble. 'The telephone upsets Queen Victoria and Disraeli terribly. Could you please text Milly to find out her intentions.'

'Right,' said Dad, 'will do. You look after yourself, Milly. See you later.'

He was out the door before you could say, who's a pretty Polly, then?

'Do you like Parrots, Milly?' Mrs Drabble asked now we were alone.

'I do, as it happens.'

Mrs Drabble frowned.

'Actually, I love Parrots.'

In fact I thought Parrots were dangerous, screeching, squawking monsters that would peck at your face as soon as look at you, but I wasn't about to share this with Mrs Drabble.

'You've come to the right place then. In fact, I'm proud say, the only house in Danemore and possibly the entire world with a Parrot from each of the five continents. Luckily we've enough rooms for this, not counting the bathroom and kitchen because keeping a Parrot there would be too messy.'

'Including Europe,' I said doubtfully.

'Including Europe. Not many know this, but the Rose-Ringed Parakeet was introduced to Britain and is now feral.'

'Feral?'

'Feral, meaning it was introduced as a pet but enough have escaped to start a colony and become naturalised. We call them the asylum seekers. If you're lucky you'll see them in parks across London.'

I didn't believe a word of what Mrs Drabble was saying, but agreed to take the tour and meet Queen Victoria and the Prince Consort, Gladstone, Disraeli and Dickens. You'll be wondering where these funny names come from. Mrs Drabble explained that because most Parrot species were discovered during the Victorian age it was decided to name the Parrots after famous Victorians. The Victorian age, in case you're wondering, lasted from 1837 to 1901 when a Queen called Victoria was on the throne. I was beginning to see why Max was so weird.

Our tour finished in the living room, where Dickens the African Grey Parrot lived.

'*Pleased to meet you.*'

At last, I thought entering the room, here's the rest of the Drabbles. But nobody was there.

'*Sit down. Make comfortable.*'

'Sorry, Mrs Drabble.'

'I didn't say anything, dear.'

Mrs Drabble was smiling.

'*Put your feet up.*'

'Then who's that?'

Mrs Drabble was laughing now.

'*Sit down. Put your feet up. Pleased to meet you.* '

'Okay, you can come out now,' Mrs Drabble said.

Dickens hopped out from behind the sofa and flapped his wings at me.

'Just one of Dickens' little games,' said Mrs Drabble, looking fondly at him.

'You mean Dickens can speak?'

'Why do you think we named him after the greatest wordsmith in the English language?'

'*Hello. Sit down. Put your feet up. Relax.*'

'But he's amazing.'

'African Grey parrots are the linguists of the Parrot family,' Mrs Drabble explained. 'Our goal for Dickens is to teach him more words than N'kisi, the current record holder, with 950 words recorded in 2004.'

'Amazing.'

'Go on, talk to Dickens. Ask him a question.'

This was silly but I had nothing to lose.

'Hello Dickens.'

'*Hello.*'

'What is your name?'

'*Dickens. What is your name?*'

'Milly. How old are you, Dickens?'

'*Nine. How old are you?*'

Mrs Drabble could forget it if she thought I was going to hold an entire conversation with a Parrot though. Time to ask a trickier question.

'Where are Mr Drabble and Max and Sandra?'

'*Out.*'

Drats. Dickens was better at this than I thought.

'I'm sorry, Milly, I should have told you earlier, but we're having so much fun. Mr Drabble and the kids have gone out.'

'Out? Out where?'

'To the hospital. Unfortunately Sandra isn't feeling very well.'

'I'm sorry to hear it. What's the matter?'

'She hasn't slept since Saturday.'

'Wow, it's Monday now. That sounds pretty serious.'

'Yes. We became so concerned after the second night that I called the doctor this morning and got an emergency appointment.'

Slime ball Max never told me this.

'So when do you expect them back?'

'They left not long before you arrived. Hopefully everything is fine and they'll be here soon. Meanwhile, let me get you a drink.'

Just my luck, but at least I won't have to hang out with Max for longer than is absolutely necessary.

'Now, what would you like?'

'But this is horrible. I mean, how is Sandra doing? She must be so tired. A glass of milk please.'

'It's pretty awful, Milly. I was with her on Saturday night and Mr Drabble stayed up with her last night. Anything else?'

'Poor girl. And a packet of Knick-Knacks if you have any.'

'Yes, unfortunately she's lost her power of speech and cries all the time. But they shouldn't be long. Right-o, I'll just pop into the kitchen. See you in a bit.'

Drats and bums. She can't even speak. There isn't much point waiting for them to get back then. I mean, at least I now have an idea of SLOB's affect on its victims, but it would have been handy to hear about Sandra's ViM and what went on in the tiny cinema. Drats and bums.

'*Relax.*'

'Yeah, yeah, it's not as easy as you think when plans fall through, Dickens.'

'*Just relax. Have a Y-not.*'

'Sorry?'

'*Why not have a Y-not.*'

Of course, there was always Dickens. Didn't Parrots repeat what they heard?

'Thanks, Dickens, but I prefer Knick-Knacks. By the way, Dickens, what's up with Sandra?'

'*Sandra don't cry.*'

'Why is Sandra crying?'

'*Sandra don't cry.*'

'Yes, but why is she crying? Okay, Dickens, let's try another way. ViMs. Nasty ViMs, ViMs fault, what's the ViM? Scary Man. Rainstorm Girl. Santa Tramp. Eazy Seats. Oh, come *on,* Dickens.'

I was running out of ideas and Mrs Drabble would be back from the kitchen soon.

'Ghost ViMs. Air Steward ViMs. Knick-Knacks.'

'*Why not have a Y-not?*

I could hear the fridge door open and shut, the crackle of a bag of crisps.

'Oh, I don't know, Dickens. I give up. Wallis in Wonderland?'

'*Not Wallis in Wonderland. Lies. Different. Guilty. Disaster.*'

'Good Dickens. Clever Dickens. Wrong film. Should have checked what was being shown in the tiny cinema. Bad parents. Too late now. Different film. What film?'

I could hear the kettle coming to the boil and water being poured out.

'*Bad film. Guilty.*'

C'mon, Milly, think, think, think…

'Jolly Dolls. Princess Dolls. Why not have a Y-not?'

'*Different film. Guilty. Disaster.*'

'You know, I think you've made a real friend there.'

I was out of time. Mrs Drabble had returned with a tray of drinks and snacks.

'You've discovered Dickens is quite the chatterbox. Milk for you,' she said, handing me the glass. 'We don't have any Knick-Knacks. Why not try of Y-not? They're new. We've just got a box of them, but they're not as good as Knick-Knacks. Fortunately they're made of maize so we're giving them to the Parrots instead.'

I picked up a Y-not from the bowl in front of me. It was exactly the same colour as Gladstone, the Red Lory Parrot from the Moluccan Islands who lived on a perch above Mr and Mrs Drabble's bed. It's a nice colour and everything, but not one you'd want to eat.

Then everybody arrived all at once except Sandra, who is staying over in hospital for further tests. In fact, Mr Drabble only stopped to drop Max off before returning 'for a bedside vigil'. I've no idea what this is, but it can't be much fun because the news is that Sandra isn't doing very well at all. Lots of important things are wrong with her and she isn't responding, though her eyes are open. She's on a drip after not eating for two days and Mr Drabble said the doctors are monitoring her progress.

Mrs Drabble cried when Mr Drabble left and Max put his arms around her and told her she'd be fine. Dad and me felt awkward and wondered what to do.

'Cup of tea?' asked Mrs Drabble when she'd recovered, though you could tell she was just being polite.

'No thanks,' said Dad. 'I think we'll just leave you in peace. Sorry to just turn up like this, but it was getting late and Milly hadn't answered my text. Unless we can help in any way, that is.'

Mrs Drabble smiled and shook her head before bursting into tears again. Max took hold of her hand and told her everything was going to be all right. He was here with her and everything was going to be all right.

'Well, it's nice to meet you, Max,' Dad said, getting up.

He then hugged me harder and longer than I can ever remember before and said we should leave. He took my hand and didn't let go until we got to the car. In the car, he didn't start the engine immediately and turned to face me.

'Mum and Dad love you and Jonas very much. You know that, don't you?'

I nodded.

'If anything happens to you or you start to feel funny in any way you'll tell us straight away, won't you?'

I nodded again.

I know this is serious, but it was hard to keep a straight face. Dad parked with the driver's side facing the street so I was able to look through his window back to the Drabble's house. All five Parrots are huddled together on the front garden. They're squawking and screaming at each other and look to be squatting, like they're sitting on eggs. Then I realise what it is they're doing. Out of each Parrot comes a bright rush of poo. Only the poo isn't white, it's Lory Parrot red.

17 Ellen's Interview

Okay, the first thing to say is that it looks like Sandra Drabble will pull through. It was touch and go for a few days, but she's definitely on the mend now. She's sleeping through the night and her appetite's returned. In fact, she polished off all the snack stoppers and third ways I brought with me when I went to see her with Max after school on Tuesday. To be honest, I was hoping she'd still be off her food or banned from eating products with high sugar content. Then I could leave half and take the rest home. Instead the doctor said the more food she got at this stage the better and she gobbled the whole lot up, leaving me with a bunch of empty wrappers and some unrecyclable packaging.

All of which would be great if she was talking, but there's little progress on that front. Tests show she can respond to pictures and identify different animals and faces, but that's about it. In other words, she's still got a long way to go. The only time she said anything was on Tuesday morning when she became very excited and screamed out cabbages three times.

Leaving the hospital I asked Max if he could think of any reason for this. Were cabbages her favourite food, or did one of the Parrots have a thing for cabbages? He couldn't think of anything, confirming my theory that cabbages must feature in the ViM Sandra experienced at SLOB. Max thought so too. In fact, Max is as angry as I am about SLOB now. First of all, he was angry about being packed off to his aunties while the rest of his family made their secret visit. Now, after I filled him in on everything, he's angry with Homemaker Industries and Fiskdale for what they've done to his baby sister.

Actually I've been spending a lot of time with Max this week. There was the hospital visit on Tuesday and Mum and Dad invited the Drabbles round for dinner on Wednesday. Then on Thursday I returned to Parrot World to swap notes with the Drabbles about SLOB. Goes without saying Mr and Mrs Drabble are as angry as Max and want to do something to stop Fiskdale. I told them the best thing they could do was tell me everything they knew, starting with how they first got in touch with SLOB. Mr Drabble was all for going round to Holbalm Hall and having it out with Fiskdale, but Max said he should leave things to me. This was nice of Max, and I've decided he's alright. I mean, sure he's a geek, but he's a brave and supportive geek.

The Drabbles contacted SLOB after seeing a tiny advert placed in Sweetland, the magazine for vintage sweet aficionados. An aficionado is a fancy foreign word for a person who knows a lot about something. For example, Mr and Mrs Drabble are Parrot aficionados, Max is an aficionado of sci-fi and fantasy books and I'm an aficionado of ballet dancing and hunky guys like John Travolta. In addition to Parrots, the Drabbles are keen collectors of sweets from the golden age of confectionary, before Health Accounts and Government restrictions began. Now I can see where Max's geekiness comes from, because being a sweet aficionado would be pretty cool if you actually got to eat the sweets. But the sorts of sweets the Drabbles collect are from so long ago they'd probably make you really sick if you ate one. For me this defeats the point, but each to their own I suppose.

Mr Drabble showed me the page in Sweetland, but the entry was so tiny that at first I couldn't find it among all the adverts for mint condition pre-Kraft Cadbury bars and first editions of rare snout fillers. There was no picture and just two lines of text.

Feeling peckish? Had enough of the kids?
Call 0776 568 453

'It so happens we were and had,' said Mr Drabble, looking at Max sheepishly, 'so I called the number.'

Mrs Drabble continued the story.

'We spoke to that nice man from the telly. You know, the tall, pale, skinny one who used to present the weather. Now he does research into babies and toddlers. Dad told him about Sandra and he said we could use their complimentary café if we let him run some tests on her for an hour. All we had to do was come in for an interview to see if Sandra was suitable. When he heard we lived in Danemore he was surprised, because the research centre is based here.'

'It was a no-brainer son,' Mr Drabble said.

'I feel so guilty,' Mrs Drabble said, bursting into tears as usual, only Max didn't go over to comfort her this time.

*

I'd worked out my next move before I got home. To my mind, there was only one family guaranteed to take up the offer advertised in Sweetland: the one Baby Ellen was in. And wasn't Mum saying I needed to be nicer to Baby Ellen? What better way than to introduce her to a world that offered sweeties on tap without hurting Auntie Mel's Health Account? But I had to work fast because I wanted this done ASAP before Eighties night next Wednesday and ideally by the weekend in order to give me enough time to get everything ready for it. And I was hoping Uncle Sid would find a way of locating something in SLOB that would make Eighties night better still. To give you a clue what this is, let me just say that Uncle Sid works as a projectionist at Danemore Picture House. A projectionist, in case you're wondering, is the person who operates the projector and makes sure everything runs smoothly at your local cinema.

As expected, Auntie Mel and Baby Ellen jumped all over the idea like hungry monkeys on a banana farm. Dad was out meeting a client on Friday so I asked Mum to invite them round for dinner, saying I was sorry about the way I treated Baby Ellen and wanted to give her a late birthday present (a very late birthday present, because her birthday's in January). Oh, and introduce her to SLOB. Mum was unsure about this after what happened to Sandra, but I told her to trust me on this one and that I knew what I was doing.

After dinner, where Baby Ellen ate about five slices of the cake Mum made especially for her, I brought out the ad from Sweetland, saying I called up myself but they were only interested in children Ellen's age. Auntie Mel snatched the magazine from my hands and rang the number to arrange to go round to Holbalm Hall for an interview the next day, Saturday the 13th of June. It crossed my mind the thirteenth wasn't the best day for my little baby cousin to meet an evil child mangler like Fiskdale, so I got them to promise not to take up any offers until they came back and reported to me first.

'Why?' protested Baby Ellen.

'Because I say so,' I said.

'That's a bit strong, Milly,' said Auntie Mel.

So I had to explain all about what happened to Sandra Drabble.

'And you expect us to expose our darling Ellen to this filth?' Uncle Sid said.

'I don't think an interview will hurt her,' I said, 'and you'll probably get a few sweeties out of it too. I know the Drabbles did. I just want to know the kind of questions Fiskdale asks. You report back, I get my information, Ellen gets some sweeties and everybody's happy.'

Then I gave Baby Ellen her birthday present, a baseball cap I had lying around that I'd fitted with a miniature microphone hidden in its lining. Obviously I didn't have a miniature microphone lying around, but I was able to get one from Marcus Watt for twenty five Slam bottles. The microphone was necessary because I didn't trust Baby Ellen or Auntie Mel one little bit, especially in situations like this where I needed them to tell the truth. I caught Uncle Sid on his way back from the loo and explained the little something extra that I needed him to do for me, saying it would help prevent another Sandra Drabble from ever happening again. Uncle Sid's a good chap and accepted his mission without asking questions.

*

Okay, it's Saturday now and Uncle Sid, Auntie Mel and Baby Ellen returned from their interview with Fiskdale just before lunchtime this morning, munching on packets of Y-nots.

'Well,' I said.

'It was pretty boring actually,' said Auntie Mel.

'Nothing to write home about,' said Uncle Sid.

'And nobody likes these Y-nots as much as Knick-Knacks either,' said Auntie Mel.

'He just asked us loads of questions then tried to persuade us to put Ellen through a series of tests in the research centre.'

'We said we'd think about it and left it at that, didn't we, Sid?'

'A pretty boring way to spend Saturday morning, although we did have a look through the area you call SLOB,' said Uncle Sid, giving me a meaningful wink.

'Thanks for nothing, yeah,' said Aunty Mel.

'My want cake,' said Baby Ellen.

After they left I rushed upstairs with the microphone I slipped out of the lining of Baby Ellen's cap when nobody was looking. Now that I've filled you in on everything that's happened, it's time to play the recording to hear how things really went. So the next voice you hear won't be mine.

'Is this it?'

Auntie Mel's voice.

'Milly saved up for three weeks to get that cap. It's her favourite.'

Mum's voice.

'And I ran it through the washing machine too.'

My voice now. Oops, I forgot. Of course it's going to run from the time I gave Baby Ellen the cap and felt for the record button in the lining. Okay, hold on a minute till I find the bit where they get to Holbalm Hall. Just fiddle your thumbs or make a Christmas list or something in the meantime. I won't be long.

Right, sorry about that. Here goes, starting with Uncle Sid.

'Well, it's certainly a big place. I always wondered who lived here.'

'Mummy, my want cake.'

'Good morning, welcome to Holbalm Hall. So glad you could make it. I'm Thomas Fiskdale, chief executive of Weatherman Industries Limited. And this is?'

'Ellen.'

'Ellen. What a lovely name. The room we'll be in is through here. Follow me please.'

'Mummy, my want cake.'

'You'll have to wait until lunch and another of your Auntie's lovely cakes darling. We've just got to talk to his nice man first.'

'Please take a seat, make yourselves comfortable. Would you like anything to drink? Tea? Coffee? I expect somebody will be round with biscuits soon.'

'My want cake.'

'I'm not sure we have any cake at the moment, Ellen. Maybe you'd like some juice. We have lots of different flavours to choose from.'

'She'll take Apple.'

'Very good. Apple it is.'

'My want cake.'

'And I'll see what I can do about cake. Now, first of all how did you find out about this opportunity?'

'We saw the advert in Sweetland.'

'Ah Sweetland, a fine publication. Well, I know the advert doesn't tell you much so let me just explain what it is we do here. Weatherman Industries is a market research company specialising in infants and babies. We think this end of the market hasn't been properly looked into because, well quite simply because infant's ideas aren't being listened to. For instance, Mister. I'm sorry, I didn't catch your name.'

'Just call me Sid.'

'Sid. And you are?'

'Mel.'

'Sid and Mel and lovely little Ellen: very good. For instance, imagine if you went shopping, Sid, and you had no say in anything you bought, from your shirts and underwear to the kind of coffee you drink?'

'He doesn't. I do all the shopping.'

'It's true I'm sorry to say, Mr Fiskdale. By the way, weren't you on the telly a few years ago.'

'Indeed I was. Presented the weather for fifteen years on the BBC. But what I'm doing now is much more important. Really giving children a voice, letting them make the consumer choices it's their absolute right to make.'

'I see.'

'So if we can borrow Ellen for just an hour while you enjoy yourselves in our complimentary café.'

'Sounds good to me. What kind of stuff do you have in this caff?'

'All kinds: coffee and pastries, cakes and sandwiches, crisps and chocolates. All donated anonymously by one of our clients as a thank you for letting us listen to what it is children really want.'

'Meantime where's Ellen?'

'Well, first of all we let the children upload a ViM in a Memory Bank capsule specially designed for little ones. This is on a subject of their choice with absolutely no direction from us. That way we can really tap into what it is little children think about and what they value. Now we all know that Memory Bank sessions are exciting but tiring, so afterwards Ellen will have some warm down time in our cinema watching Wallis In Wonderland.'

'That's a good one.'

'Thanks, Mel, we think so too. Finally you join up with Ellen to enter a booth designed to look like a real consumer environment where she can choose between different products and tell us why she made her choices. And that's it. All you need to do on the way out is sign a form for legal purposes and we'll give you a box of goodies to go away with.'

'Well that all sounds fine, doesn't it, Mel. There's just one little thing before we agree to this. I'd like to have a look over the place, just to see that it's a safe environment for Ellen. She's never been in a cinema on her own, for instance. If I'm satisfied than I'm sure we have a deal, Mr Fiskdale.'

'But of course, Sid, I understand your concern. If you follow me, and I'll maybe ask you and Ellen a few questions on our way over.'

'Fire away.'

'Mind the door, by the way. Weatherman Industries is in the middle of a refit at the moment, so we have to go through this little cupboard to reach the research centre.'

'My want cake, mister.'

'Ah, I see you've spotted all the goodies on the shelves here. I suppose we have time for a quick look. Pick anything you see, Ellen, and as long as your mummy is happy with your choice it's yours.'

'My want two.'

'And two you shall have, Ellen. Anything you want really, as long as Mummy is happy about it. What a delightful child you have there, Mel, and while she's choosing let me just ask you a few questions...'

Drats and bums. The tape just ran out.

All is not lost though, because I called Uncle Sid to find out if his wink meant what I thought it did. Bingo! He managed to grab one of the discs featuring what was shown in the tiny cinema and hide it under his jumper. Thank goodness he never got searched on the way out, but I guess they don't want to embarrass all these Mums and Dads who've been busy trousering goodies in the café.

'Excellent, Uncle Sid. You're my favourite, most amazing Uncle ever.'

'That wouldn't be too hard, Milly. You've only got one.'

'Oh all right, but you're still number one. By the way, I never got around to asking you, what did Fiskdale ask you about Ellen?'

'Oh, just to confirm her age, what our household income was, what her favourite toys were, etcetera. Stuff like that.'

'And I know you did this already, but promise me again you're not going back to put Ellen through all those horrid tests.'

'We're not going to do that, Milly, especially after what happened to that poor girl you told us about.'

'Very good.'

'And we wouldn't have time anyway. Mr Fiskdale said today is the final day he's going to run the unit.'

'What?'

'Yeah, he said the work was done and it was time to pack up and move on.'

Crikey. There's not a minute to lose then.

18 Eighties Night

It's Tuesday night now and the past few days have been crazy. Not just for me, but for Jonas and Max Drabble, Mum and Dad and Uncle Sid too, and even Budi Noors, who only landed a few hours ago. Which is just as well, because there's a lot to do and not much time, with only four days between Uncle Sid bringing me the tiny cinema films on Saturday and Eighties night tomorrow. Luckily everybody's keen to lend a hand because of what happened to poor Sandra Drabble. And nobody's got anything better to do after Dad's team lost the World Cup final and Vladimir the Vanquisher whipped Jonas. I never did tell you Dad's team, did I? That's because he went and supported a country he's never even been to, which I don't think is very cool, and loads worse than Jonas wearing his Allez France scarf for French games. I mean, at least Jonas has visited France and speaks some French. I just think Dad was sick of supporting teams on the losing side, so it's kind of cruel things worked out like that anyway. To give you a clue, the first letter of Dad's team is B, it ends with an L and has got a Z in the middle, or an S if you're actually from that country. So it'll be a Z for Dad then.

Anyway, as I said, all systems are go here. Which makes it all the more frustrating Max and me have to waste valuable time at school rehearsing Eighties sketches we're never going to perform, though Max makes a better fairytale Prince than King Charles ever did. Every P7 is getting five minutes, so there's a long evening ahead. Hopefully not everybody will use the full five minutes because Max and me are at the end and need all the time we can get. Our plan is to perform ViMs from Fiskdale's Memory Bank, alongside tiny cinema films featuring the same characters. This is possible because the disk Uncle Sid took from SLOB contains the films running from R to Z, including Santa Tramp, Rainstorm Girl and Volcano Man, plus a couple of others. Volcano Man, by the way, is the name Fiskdale gave Jonas' Scary Man ViM. Uncle Sid said there were also disks A to H and I to Q, but remembered me mentioning Rainstorm Girl so plumped for R to Z. Thank goodness, because if he took any of the others there's no way we could do this.

The disk lasts twenty minutes, the same length of time the little ones were in the tiny cinema. Fiskdale's plan must be to have Memory Bank sessions with these ViMs, show the related films and then assess their impact in the observation booths. Twenty minutes divided by five equals four minutes per film, or twelve minutes for three, which still makes two minutes more than we've got. After examining a photo of the site, Uncle Sid said there's no problem because he could play the films concurrently rather than consecutively. I've no idea what this means, so it's just as well he brought extra projectors along to run all three films at the same time during our dress rehearsal at Danemore Picture House after school today. Apparently the stage at school is large enough for three small scenes with the films playing directly above on repeat. The next worry is that performing three ViMs simultaneously will confuse the audience, so Uncle Sid designed a mobile lighting unit to spotlight them in turn. The upshot of all this is that everything looked sensational during the run through. Between you and me, I think Uncle Sid's wasted as a cinema projectionist and should really be directing big-budget blockbusters.

On more familiar territory, Mum finished my Eighties wedding dress on Sunday and went on to make a Volcano Man cape for Budi Noors and Adrian Gulp's tramp clothes to fit under Max's Santa costume. Thankfully these costumes are a lot simpler to put together and were ready in time for the dress rehearsal. Meantime, in the garage, Dad's been making props. He found the Volcano Man and Rainstorm Girl scenes pretty easy because they're both outside and just need a few trees dotted about. But Santa Tramp's a lot more work and Dad's got us wrapping stuff up to put under the plastic Christmas tree he borrowed from the Drabbles. He painted a kitchen chair gold for Santa's throne and even made a reindeer out of paper mache to sit by Santa's side just like I said it did in the ViM. Finally he decked everything out with Mum's box of Christmas decorations and made a Good Green Energy Grotto sign large enough to be seen from the back of the hall.

Jonas got the day off school to welcome Budi, and filled him in on what's happening after thanking him for bringing a suitcase of coffee over for Dad. They rehearsed their scene after lunch to have everything ready for the run through. Mum plays the Audrey Campbell character running me over in Rainstorm Girl, with special sound affects of screeching wheels and screaming provided by Uncle Sid and Baby Ellen.

Finally, we've got Tom Crabb reliving his finest moment in Santa Tramp, with Dad playing the Delice-Stanley-Bahm character and Max in the Adrian Gulp role. In other words, it looks like everything's ready, though I'm pretty nervous about how things will work out on the night. After all, what Max and me have in store is nothing like what we're supposed to be doing. There'll be lots of infants in the audience too, little brothers and sisters like Sandra and Baby Ellen. At first I thought this was a good thing because their reaction will highlight SLOB's evilness, but now I'm more worried about *how* they'll react.

Not to mention the bigger picture, something Mrs Lolly always tells us to think about at school. It's true I've found out loads in the past few weeks, but there's still a lot I don't understand and many questions left unanswered. Above all, will Amy and Sandra Drabble and the other infants and babies who visited SLOB ever get better? This is the biggie, but there are lots of other things niggling me too. Like, what's so special about Volcano Man? Jonas asked Budi this and Budi said in Indonesia there are spirits all over the place and most people believe most things. Which isn't exactly what Jonas wanted to hear after finally getting the whole Fiskdale semi-being story settled in his mind. Unfortunately when he explained this to Budi, Budi said he wouldn't be surprised if semi-beings existed either. I even got the feeling Budi was a little anxious about playing Volcano Man, but he hid it well. So was this why I felt sick seeing Adrian Gulp playing Volcano Man, just as Jonas had with the real Volcano Man? Was even pretending to be a semi-being dangerous? And what about Rainstorm Girl and all those sightings of Hannah Dyson? Maybe ghosts really do exist after all. I don't know. There are just too many questions buzzing around my brain at the moment.

At least I found out that Stiehls, the makers of Rhapsody seats, is a Homemaker Industries company and Eazy Seats are made by Montgomery-Robb, Stiehls biggest competitors. Equally Princess Dolls are made by Tandy Enterprises, which is a Homemaker Industries company, and Jolly Dolls aren't. I even discovered why the little girl in the SLOB booth stuffed the Jolly Dolls to the back of the shelves, after watching the tiny cinema film for Volcano Man. Actually I reckon this film is the best one I've seen yet, which maybe explains why Fiskdale was so keen to get his hands on Jonas' ViM. It's set on a beach just like Volcano Man, though the grey skies and lack of palm trees suggest we're not exactly on the same beach. It's hard to tell whether Adrian Gulp plays Volcano Man or not, but the time Jonas saw Volcano Man in the Secret Room must have been a rehearsal because I doubt even invisible rooms can fit real beaches inside them.

Volcano Man sits in front of a bonfire with several Jolly Dolls beside him. He picks up a Jolly Doll in one hand and a knitting needle in the other. The scene switches to earlier on the same beach. A few little girls are making sandcastles when Volcano Man wanders into view, but their reaction is very different from Jonas's because instead of being scared they find his old-fashioned cape funny and start giggling. Back to the bonfire scene, where Volcano Man stabs the knitting needle right through the Jolly Doll's heart and throws it on the bonfire. Over to the giggling girls, who are now holding their sides and screaming in pain before throwing themselves onto their sandcastles. Volcano Man smiles and picks up another Jolly Doll, leading to a similar torture scene featuring children playing football who kick the ball in his face, and a third with little girls splashing water at him. After watching these scenes it's no wonder the little girl in the booth wanted the Jolly Dolls out of sight. And it's no wonder Sandra Drabble has ended up the way she is. I mean this stuff could give a grown up nightmares for years, so goodness knows what it'll do to babies and toddlers.

This is on Mum's mind too, and the reason she called Amy's mum to ask if we could use Amy to show what happens when you introduce ViMs to very young children. But the ViM she saw isn't anything like these, I pointed out. 'Exactly,' Mum said, 'which just goes to show the effect ViMs have on little ones even when they're relatively harmless.' I wish I could experience the ViM of Fiskdale's interview with the BBC now. To my mind Amy seeing this was either an accident that gave Fiskdale his evil plan, or Amy was a test case from the days before he built up his library of more harmful ViMs. Anyway Amy's mum didn't want to know until Mum filled her in on Fiskdale and SLOB and what happened to Sandra Drabble. Now she's happy to do anything to help, so Amy's going to be up there on stage with Sandra Drabble, after Sandra's mum persuaded the hospital to let her out for a few hours.

So all that's left for me to do now is write a speech explaining things before the action starts. At least I'll be wearing my Eighties wedding dress, so I'll look the part. The thing is, I'm not very good at writing stuff down, so I'll try it out on you first and see what you think. Okay, here goes nothing.

'Good evening, ladies and gentlemen, and welcome to the final performance of the night. I hope you've had a good time on your trip down memory lane and I'm sure you want Max and me to get on with it, but what we're doing needs an explanation first because it's a little different. For the past few months I've been on the trail of something very fishy happening right here in Danemore and I'm using tonight to share what I've found with you. You'll find it strange at first, then hopefully interesting and finally upsetting enough to want to rise up and do something about. What you'll see is Max and me and a few others acting out three ViMs from the Memory Bank. Why? Because these ViMs are being experienced by very young children in a special room in Holbalm Hall. And directly afterwards they'll go into a tiny cinema to watch the same films you'll see projected above you on the stage tonight.

Okay, so what's my point? Well, in the projected films you'll clearly be able to make out products like Knick-Knacks, Eazy Seats and Jolly Dolls. This is no accident, because what we have here is the most evil kind of advertising, which is really anti-advertising, designed to turn your baby sons and daughters into lifelong consumers of certain products through a system of fear and brain mangling.'

At this point Sandra and Amy join me on stage and do their thing, including lots of stammering and shaking and blank staring.

'So I'm taking the opportunity of using this public audience of parents and guardians who want the very best for their children to show up Mr Thomas Fiskdale, Holbalm Hall and Homemaker Industries for what they really are: dangerous child mangling crooks who need to be stopped *right now*. Thank you for your time. Enjoy the rest of the show.'

*

So Eighties night happened yesterday and everything went to plan. Apart from the audience reaction, that is, which was lukewarm with bewilderment rather than boiling with rage. At least we managed to get right through to the end because I'd slipped a sleeping pill into our headteacher's water bottle. But I'm just so disappointed with how things turned out, especially after a few toddlers in the audience started screaming in fear. I don't understand how so many men and women, some with children the age of Fiskdale's target audience, could be so unaffected by the experience. I guess people just wanted to get home after a long night. Maybe we should have gone on at the beginning or something. I don't know. It's just all so disappointing and to be honest I feel kind of low.

But it's not really for me to comment on how the evening went. I'll leave that to the evening edition of The Danemore Post, which has just popped through the letterbox and carries a full-page report on page seven. Most of this is taken up with a picture of Sarah Fiddle in her stupid Madonna outfit, but at least there's a paragraph. Let me read it to you now.

Back to the Future

Danemore Primary Students go all Eighties

Danemore Primary School was packed to the rafters last night when Primary 7 pupils put on their end of year show celebrating the best of the Eighties. A lively audience sang along to acts including Michael Jackson, Madonna and Wham, and Eddie Murphy, the Blues Brothers and the Two Ronnies had them roaring down the aisles. Top Gun was Jake Barnacle as Tom Cruise and Rex Stevens was Footloose as a big city kid in a small town, with Casper and Cassie Cruise putting an interesting spin on Bros. A long and enjoyable evening was topped off with sweethearts Lady Diana and Prince Charles, otherwise known as Milly Buntly and Max Drabble, tying the knot. We wish the Royal Couple a happy future and look forward to a reunion show soon.

What! That's not right! That's rubbish! There's something wrong there, but after all the effort of last night and the past few months I don't really care any more. I'm tired and it's time to end this silly habit of recording stuff nobody's ever going to hear. Oh, and I'd just like to say a big thank you to the people of Danemore for supporting me and taking an interest in what I've uncovered. I don't know. Maybe I'll go back to Indonesia with Budi Noors. At least they don't have Memory Banks and Health Accounts there, and the papers probably aren't rigged either. Anyway, that's it for me. Good night, God bless and don't let the semi-beings bite.

19 Out Of Reach

The weekend started really early today and by the time I was fully awake and realised what was happening I didn't mind one little bit. I think it was the front gate clattering that stirred me to go down and investigate. I usually don't hear this but early morning noises are different, so a mouse can become a lion and a few people out in the street sound like an army on the march. Which made it all the more amazing to unlock the door and find an actual army on the doorstep. Marcus Watt's dad was at the front.

'Good morning, Milly, just the girl we're looking for. Sorry to get you up so early, but we decided this couldn't wait. We're going round to Mr Fiskdale's now and were wondering if you'd like to come along.'

'What, yeah, sure.'

I looked at the mass of people crowding the front garden and extending down the road as far as I could see in both directions. Faces familiar and not so familiar, parents and grandparents, students and teenagers, babies and toddlers, kids my own age. Some in pyjamas and dressing gowns like they're not long out of bed, others in regular clothes, or work clothes if they'd just got off the night shift. A few of the old timers even wore jackets and ties. They carried hoes and rakes and pans, walking sticks, hockey sticks and tennis rackets. Signs and banners with slogans saying

STOP SLOB, Danemore Parent's Association says NO to Baby Mangling and Y-Not P-Off Fiskdale fluttered above. Many had on baseball caps with the Homemaker Industries' logo crossed out like the Ghostbusters t-shirt Algernon Savage wore on Eighties night. Almost all were looking in my direction.

'No, I mean, what's this about?'

'The citizens of Danemore are taking a stand. Following your advice, we're actually going to do something about Fiskdale and Holbalm Hall.'

'What? Sorry, I'm kind of slow in the mornings. Could you say all that again?'

'Is it okay if we discuss the finer points on the way over, Milly? After all, it'd be a shame to get all these people up just to hang out in your front garden.'

'Sure. Okay, let me just get dressed first.'

It was all Marcus Watt's dad's idea. He'd been as disappointed by the non-reaction at Eighties night as I was. His barbershop didn't open until ten thirty, so on Thursday morning he had time to call other parents and get their thoughts, with always the same response. Yes it was shocking and yes it had to be stopped, but what chance a few locals against the might of Homemaker Industries. And anyway, nobody was forcing these young girls and boys to visit Holbalm Hall. The responsibility was with the parents, not Homemaker Industries. It sounded like a cop out to Mr Watt, who then asked how they felt after the show and was again stuck by how similar the answers were. More than a few mentioned being stunned into silence and feeling sick and helpless, like how people do about global warming or nuclear weapons. Many slept badly or had nightmares about brides in Eighties dresses and hooded figures with Voodoo Jolly Dolls. Those with young kids were up half the night trying to settle them. After some prompting, most agreed they felt angry and something had to be done. Mr Watt closed his shop for the day and called an emergency meeting of Danemore Parents' Association.

Not one member missed the meeting, despite it being during the day in the middle of the week. After much discussion, two things were decided. First, there should be a boycott of all Homemaker Industries products and pressure put on the Mayor to make Danemore the first Homemaker Industries-free town. Secondly, there should be a demonstration outside Holbalm Hall this weekend and maybe one outside the London headquarters of Homemaker Industries UK too. When the meeting broke up members called their friends and these friends called other friends and soon everybody in Danemore knew about the planned demo. Everybody, that is, except me.

Scrambling upstairs to get dressed ASAP I caught sight of Mum, Dad and Jonas having breakfast in the kitchen. They were already dressed and ready for the march. Jonas had even made a sign with Fiskdale's spidery arms holding the bars of a prison cell and Justice scrawled in bright Lory Parrot Red below. Actually the words had run slightly and I wondered whether this was intentional or Jonas was too impatient to wait for the paint to dry before holding the sign up to see how it looked. Either way, it was pretty cool.

'What?' I said. 'You too!'

'C'mon, Milly,' said Jonas, stuffing the last bit of a bacon roll into his gob, 'you know what a blabbermouth you are.'

They'd known from the beginning. Dad even wrote the article I'd read in the Danemore Post to keep Fiskdale off the scent. Blimey!

At least I'd put my thinking cap on when I got dressed, because the final thing I did before joining everybody outside was to give Moses a good sniff of the disk from the tiny cinema and put his lead on to join us. I reckoned we might very well end up entering Holbalm Hall and Moses might lead us to places we'd miss, which turned out to be a stroke of genius, if I say so myself.

*

'This is great,' said Dad, right about the time I got my first blister.

'What's great about it?' I asked. 'I don't see why we have to actually *walk* there. Can't we hire busses or get taxis or something.'

'That would ruin the great tradition of civil protest, Milly. We are following in the proud footsteps of the Peasant's Revolt of 1381, the Jarrow Marchers in the Great Depression and Mao Zedong on his Long March.'

'What? Who's Mao Zedong?'

'You must have heard of Chairman Mao, Milly, leader of the Chinese People's Liberation Army.'

'No I haven't. And I'm not Chinese or a Peasant or from Jarrow, wherever that is. Or depressed for that matter. I'm just a twelve-year-old girl from Danemore.'

'Are we almost there yet, Dad? Please tell us we're almost there,' said Jonas.

'My want cake,' said Baby Ellen from her pram.

It was time to move groups, and Moses and me soon fell in with the Drabbles. Sandra had been given her first overnight stay from hospital to be able to go on this march and Max was pushing her in the pram and being his usual sweet self, singing her favourite songs and playing I spy.

'Shouldn't you be with your family?' he asked.

'No, it's boring and they're all being very annoying. Anyway, I'd much rather be here with you.'

I don't know where this came from and I wasn't even sure if I meant it. Then Max gave me one of his lovely smiles and I realised I did mean it after all. I took over pushing the pram because Max was in his funny Star Wars costume that he likes to wear on the weekends and was beginning to overheat. John Travolta he wasn't. Who would have thought it, that I'd fall for the biggest geek at school. I just hoped he still liked me a little bit too.

The sun was high in the sky by the time we reached Holbalm Hall and our numbers seemed to have doubled or trebled on the way. It was a lovely day and a party atmosphere was starting. There were stalls at the gates selling tofu, lentils and beanburgers. Jugglers, buskers and street artists kept the crowds entertained. Some bright spark even brought a couple of portable toilets and was charging an entrance fee in non-Homemaker Industries sweets. Why wasn't I surprised when I learned Marcus Watt was behind this? But at the same time I was touched to see he had another bucket for Homemaker Industries products to be handed in and sent to people in need in the poorer parts of the world. As a result of this hullabaloo I was worried Fiskdale would skip over the wall and escape, but a human chain quickly formed around the estate singing songs and doing the biggest Hokey Cokey I'd ever seen. They must have looked like some strange noisy multicoloured millipede on Google Live Cam. When I cut through the crowds to reach the front I was handed a loudspeaker by Marcus Watt's dad and encouraged to say something.

'Don't worry,' he said, 'they'll hear inside. I've rigged up a number of speakers around the entrance so Fiskdale doesn't miss a thing.'

A terrible shyness overcame me and I handed the loudspeaker back.

'Look, Mr Watt,' I said, 'there's no point because he'll never come out and he's got enough snack stoppers and third ways inside to last him for years. If he's even still there. Because you see that For Sale sign on the turret up there? Well, that wasn't there last week. No, I think the only thing to do is break in.'

'What?' said Mr Watt. 'But that's against the law. We'll be lowering ourselves to the level of these crooks.'

'Let's make this protest a peaceful one, Milly,' said Dad, who'd arrived with Mum and Jonas. I was pleased to see they'd managed to lose Auntie Mel and Baby Ellen, but sad not to see Uncle Sid with them, my Eighties night hero.

But somebody must have overheard me because there were loud murmurings in the crowd and a slow chant of 'break in, break in, break in' began. The crowd started to heave and swell like how tectonic plates must do before volcanoes erupt. The only problem was that we were in the Ring of Fire bit, pressed up against the big wooden doors.

'Breath in,' said Mr Watt, 'and cover your head. I think you're just about to get your wish.'

The next few hours were complete chaos, a blur of noise and colour and bodies and flashing lights and Police sirens. Nobody had ever been inside Holbalm Hall before, although many had lived in its shadow for years. Now it was time to wander and explore, swim in the lake, get lost in the maze, climb the turrets. Needless to say Fiskdale was nowhere to be seen and there was no trace of SLOB either. As far as I could tell, Holbalm Hall had lost its spooky virtuality and was entirely back to its old self, but there was nothing in it now. Fiskdale had really gone, packed up and moved on, just like he told Uncle Sid he would. I don't think he'll be getting a quick sale though, not after the way things were left at the end of the day. Hopefully Homemaker Industries are paying for repairs.

*

There's just one other thing to mention before I do finally leave you for good this time. You might remember at the beginning of this wonderful, magical day my saying that I'd brought Moses

along, and that bringing him along was a stroke of genius.
Anyway, after things quietened down in the afternoon and Max
and me were sunbathing on the lawn, Moses got all excited and
started straining his lead to return to the area where the Secret
Room and SLOB had been. Actually, I'd kind of forgotten why
I'd brought Moses along by that time and was a little irritated
about this, especially when I was finally getting some quality time
with Max.

But you ignore Moses at your peril and where he leads you
follow. He stopped in an area directly behind Fiskdale's sweet
cupboard, which I'm guessing would have been where the
corridor into the secret rooms was. In fact I was still able to tell
where these buildings had been from two rectangles of shorter
grass on the ground. But it was in the longer grass that Moses
started sniffing and burrowing. And right enough, there did seem
to be a patch of grass coloured differently to the rest, like it had
recently been dug up and re-laid.

After several minutes of Max and me digging and Moses
burrowing we came across the outline of something hard and
square and metallic. A few more minutes and we were sitting
staring at a small metal box the shape and size of the coffee
containers Dad gets from the Noors. But it was padlocked, with a
thick metal chain wrapped around it.

'Have no fear,' said Max, pulling out a space age looking hammer
from a pocket on the belt on his Star Wars costume, 'Intergalactic
travellers are always prepared.'

After a lot of manly hammering and wrenching and box
bludgeoning, Max prised the thing open. So what was in it? Well
for one thing, nothing like what we thought would be in it.

Nothing like what we thought would be in it *in our wildest dreams*. I mean, sure it was Fiskdale's box, and sure it had everything to do with what we'd been investigating. But at the same time it had nothing to do with what we'd been investigating. In fact, it took our breath away. The contents of the box took our breath away.

So what was in it then? Well, I've not even told Mum and Dad or Jonas yet, so I'm not exactly going to tell you first, am I? But what's in the box makes everything so much bigger, bigger than you could ever imagine in your *wildest* dreams.

Lightning Source UK Ltd.
Milton Keynes UK
171854UK00001B/14/P